HILL SPIRITS V

An Anthology by Writers
of five counties in Eastern Ontario

Editor
Susan Statham

blue denim press

Published by Blue Denim Press Inc.
Cover Art: John Charlton. Cover Design: Shane Joseph
Editor: Susan Statham. Copy Editor: Christopher Cameron
Published in Canada
ISBN 978-1-927882-79-5

Library and Archives Canada Cataloguing in Publication
Title: Hill spirits.
Names: Sidnell Reid, Felicity, 1936- editor. | Scheltema, Gwynn, 1954- editor. | Statham, Susan,
    1951- editor. | Rummel, Erika, 1942- editor.
Description: First edition. | Volume V edited by Susan Statham. | Volume 5 has subtitle: An anthology
    by writers of five counties in Eastern Ontario.
Identifiers: Canadiana (print) 20129053813 | Canadiana (ebook) 20129053821 | ISBN 9781927882795 (v. 5 ; softcover) |
    ISBN 9781927882801 (v. 5 ; Kindle) | ISBN 9781927882818 (v. 5 ; EPUB)
Subjects: LCSH: Canadian literature—Ontario—Northumberland. | LCSH: Canadian literature—Ontario,
    Eastern. | LCSH: Canadian literature—21st century. | CSH: Canadian literature (English)—Ontario—
    Northumberland. | CSH: Canadian literature (English)—Ontario, Eastern | CSH: Canadian literature
    (English)—21st century.
Classification: LCC PS8255.O5 H55 2012 | DDC C810.8/0971357—dc23

"We know what we are,
but know not what we may be."
—William Shakespeare

Welcome

Join us in **Celebrating Resilience** through this fine selection of short stories, poems and personal narratives. Resilience is the ability to bend and flex like a tree in a violent storm, to persevere like a flower pushing through the pavement of a parking lot and in the words of a Japanese proverb to "fall seven times and stand up eight."

We have all faced life's difficulties. Like you, our writers have overcome adversity, loss, disappointment, misfortune, heartache and the first global pandemic in over a century. There is inspiration in their words of resilience—expressed often with humour, sometimes with sorrow and always with resolve.

The launch of this anthology marks the first year for the Northumberland Festival of the Arts, an expansion of the 2017 and 2019 Spirit of the Hills Festival of the Arts. *Hill Spirits V* reflects this expansion with literary contributions from writers across five counties in Eastern Ontario: Northumberland, Durham, Peterborough, Hastings and Prince Edward.

Many thanks to the writers who, with strength and wisdom, through fiction and nonfiction, have shared some of their lowest lows and highest highs. And a special note of gratitude for the professional copy editing of Christopher Cameron.

Susan Statham, Editor

Table of Contents

Jessica Outram

MY FIRST BORN GARDEN

It's easy to think of reasons to wait
for money, time, help: a green thumb

lost in blogs about seeds
when to plant, where to place, how to protect

avoid daily watering, weeding
watch for invaders while waiting for harvest

until one day I stop
plan, think, wonder: resist

seeds into soil
hot sun beams as I unwind the hose from its web

cardinals sing surprise in the forsythia
until it's done

I rest in the plastic lawn chair by the soil
like a parent watching a newborn sleep.

Catherine White

THE SHAPE OF THINGS TO COME

I am trying to age gracefully, but events conspire and I confess to not being terribly successful at it. The other day I bought a lovely blue sweater with sequins, a bit form-fitting but not too extreme. Just the sort of subdued thing that a lady my age could wear to a wedding, like the one I have to attend next week. Of course, the weddings I attend now are mostly for people's grandchildren. No one's looking at me anyway when there is much better scenery around. But one must try to do one's best. Who knows if an old beau might turn up? You wouldn't want him to think you had let yourself go.

The sweater looked just fine until I got it home. Then, would you believe, when I tried it on, all of a sudden there were these well-defined rolls around my waist and at my back. Where on earth had they come from? That's what I want to know. I am sure they weren't there in the morning—but there they were, bold as brass. No matter how I tried to straighten up, they would not go away. I certainly must try to view myself from different angles in the future. These rolls are particularly unsightly, but it was too late to try to lose them a week before the wedding.

After that shock, I decided to have a really good look at myself in the mirror. I needed to know what was what; but I don't recommend that approach until you have had a good strong drink. Alcohol might just soften your vision a bit, which in my case would have been a blessing.

In the cold clear light of the bathroom mirror it seemed, to my amazement, that everything was six inches lower than it used to be. Again I wondered, when did that begin to happen? The pleasure in buying that new sweater was wearing off quickly.

Undaunted, I decided that there was nothing to do but to go out and purchase a new "foundation" as our grandmothers used to call it. Off to the stores I went with great confidence—a woman on a mission.

Of course, the lingerie on display is meant for girls, not mature women, so I accosted a sales clerk and explained the dilemma. She was quite nice about it. She suggested a garment called Spanx. The name, I thought, was a bit off-putting, but the reality was even worse.

Into the dressing room I was herded, like a lamb to the slaughter, with this little garment in my hand. And it did seem little, even though the tag stated the size was XXL. Surely it must have been mislabelled? There were no instructions, so the first dilemma was this: how was one actually supposed to wear the thing? Exactly what part of the anatomy was it supposed to work on?

I stripped to the waist—with unflattering lights and a three-way mirror for cold comfort—and started to wriggle into the thing. I can only believe that Spanx must surely be made out of Goodyear tires, and I must say, are just about as flexible. It wouldn't pull up over my derriere, and in fact, got sort of stuck until I peeled it off with a huge effort, trying not to pant and puff, as the clerk was just outside the changing room door asking how I was getting on.

"Not at all," I told her, "but I'm working on it."

Changing tactics, I pulled it over my head; but again, the blasted thing got stuck before I could get my shoulders enclosed. It took an amazing feat of strength to finally get it where it was apparently supposed to be and the result was, shall we say, surprising.

First, I could barely breathe and thought I was in a Victorian nightmare that would soon involve the vapours and smelling salts. Secondly, and most amazingly, my breasts had disappeared! I could not find them anywhere. No need to worry about any sagging in that department. I finally discovered that they were flattened out and seemed to be in my armpits—not at all a satisfactory result and certainly not the image I was after.

I might mention that I did feel that the rolls had disappeared, but then I was afraid to look behind me to see where they had descended to. I imagined it would involve a larger pair of trousers.

"I don't think this will do for me," I called out to the sales clerk through the door.

She gave a sort of sniff and said she had nothing else to suggest except perhaps a larger sweater.

I felt that the remark was a bit rude, but young people can be like that sometimes. I do suppose she had a point, but by then I was completely out of sorts and in no mood to hear that type of advice.

I will leave it to your imagination to visualize the goings on inside that tiny change room in order for me to get out of that hideous piece of modern elastic. Suffice it to say, a slingshot comes to mind. Finally free, I can tell you that I was totally relieved to find that all my bits and pieces, albeit somewhat creased, returned to their rightful location—however disagreeable that location may be.

I have decided to persevere. Rolls be damned, I will wear the sweater to the wedding anyway. And when it comes to dancing, I'll find some old gent who likes substantial women. Clearly, aging is a social skill, the etiquette of which I will need to explore further.

Alice McMurtry

AERIAL COMBAT

looping, frenzied
her chick in foe's talons
sparrow jousts falcon
staring at curved beak

openness of failure
feathers fanned
the cries hover
minute war unfolds
spoils unwon

she shakes off mantle
returns to clutch
she knows no numbers
but feels something taken
ageless the turning of seasons

Susan Statham

STAY

It happened on an evening much the same as any other, until suddenly it wasn't. Julia was propped on the sofa ready for her favourite sitcom. Tuppence lay curled up in the small space created by one bent knee.

When Julia shifted her right leg, the motion prompted the French bulldog to raise her head. Her greying muzzle caught the rays of sunlight refracting through the large picture window and she pushed herself up with her front paws. Then she fell over onto her side.

"Whoa, Tups," said Julia, putting two hands around the dog's chest, lifting and turning Tuppy to face her. "What seems to be ...?" Words failed when she saw her dog's eyes bouncing back and forth like a metronome. Thinking it might be the result of accidentally forcing Tuppy to look into the sun, Julia carried her to the carpeted front hall and carefully set her down on all four feet.

"Are you okay, old girl?" she asked. Like a novice sailor on a rough sea, Tuppy took a few wobbly steps, vomited, and collapsed. "Ohmygod, ohmygod." The little dog seemed barely conscious and Julia was sure her pet was having a stroke. "Stay with me Tuppy," she begged as she scooped her up, ran out the front door, across the street, down a block and a half and pounded on Madeline's door.

"It'll be okay. It'll be okay," she promised and petted until the door opened.

"Something's wrong with Tuppence," Julia told Scott. "Is Maddie here?"

"Yeah," Scott looked over his shoulder to the staircase, "but she's leaving for the clinic in a few—"

Julia walked past him to the bottom of the stairs. "Maddie," she called and the young veterinarian appeared at the upper landing. "Tuppy's sick. Can you look at her?"

Madeline had been their vet until her son was born. Following her maternity leave, she left the local practice for part-time work at an out-of-town emergency clinic. Julia always told herself she would never impose on her neighbour and never had, but at 7:30 on a Friday night her options were limited.

As Maddie descended the stairs, Scott ducked into the living room and Julia, panicked by the unknown, poured out a description of Tuppy's symptoms. On the lower landing the vet, relaxed by the familiar, took the pup's face in her cupped hands. Noting the rapid eye movement she said, "This is nystagmus. In humans it can indicate a stroke, but in dogs it's generally related to vestibular disease."

"This is a disease?" asked Julia. Tears, like raindrops on a pane of glass, slid down her cheeks.

"A misnomer. It's actually more like a syndrome. And you said she vomited?"

Julia nodded and Maddie gently lifted the dog from her arms. "Is Tuppence eleven or twelve?"

Brushing the tears away with the tips of her fingers she whispered, "She's fourteen."

Maddie's eye's widened but she said nothing. Supporting the little dog under her chest and belly, the vet lowered her onto the large mat by the front door. Tuppy stood, listing like a boat taking on water. Despite a little prompting, she refused to walk. Maddie picked her up and handed her back to Julia. "I'm sure Tuppence has what is often called old dog vertigo."

"Vertigo," echoed Julia. "So she's dizzy?"

"That's right."

"Is that why she seems so lost and detached?"

Maddie nodded. "The only world Tuppence has ever known doesn't exist right now. It's topsy turvy and she can't find her place in it."

"And when will things go back to normal?" Julia asked.

Maddie compressed her lips and shrugged. "Most dogs recover within a couple of weeks, though many retain that head tilt. It could be the world never completely goes back to what it was."

"*Most* dogs recover?"

"Try not to worry." Maddie patted her arm, then raised an index finger. "I have something that might help. I'll be right back." The vet returned with a blister pack in one hand and a small plastic syringe in the other. "This is anti-nausea medication, and if Tuppy won't drink, use this syringe. Place the plastic end in the water and pull up the plunger to draw it into the barrel. Then lift her flew, basically her upper lip, and simply insert and squirt into the side of her mouth. It's really important to keep her hydrated."

Accepting the meds and syringe and slipping them into the back pocket of her jeans, Julia apologized for not bringing her purse. Maddie waved away any talk of payment. "Get some rest and like I said, try not to worry. Dogs are resilient."

Julia nodded, recalling Tuppy's stoic silence when she lost most of a toenail caught in a vent cover. A scratched cornea meant frequent eyedrops and two weeks in the "cone of shame," but the little dog soldiered on like it was a minor inconvenience. At age four, she miraculously survived an emergency spay. But ten years later, did she have the strength and the will to fight this?

Feeling grateful yet anxious, Julia carried her sick girl home and lowered her to the hall carpet. For a few seconds, the little Frenchie stood firm but soon swayed like a hippo in a wave pool. Julia got on her knees, and cradling her companion, rubbed her face into the soft fur of the dog's neck and wept. "I love you, Tuppy. Please stay with me."

Tuppence had only been crated for the first few months of her life. This meant she'd spent years sleeping on her human mom's bed. Not just on the bed, but on the bed pressed next to Julia. The dog was like a heat seeking missile and Julia often awoke in the morning one roll away from falling off the edge. It was like that nonsense verse—*There were ten on the bed and the little one said, "Rollover, rollover."* One falls out with each turn until only the little one remains. Watching her best friend try to navigate the few feet in front of her, she knew it would be the little one that rolled off first.

Leaving Tuppence in the kitchen, Julia pulled her foam mattress from its bed frame and dragged it into her home office. For the next little while, they would be sleeping on the floor. To provide her pup with better traction, she laid a runner at the foot of the mattress and two small carpets on either side.

Returning to the kitchen, Julia took the blister pack from her back pocket. Any previously prescribed pills had either been added to food or happily consumed hidden in a piece of cheese. Given Tuppy's muddled state, Julia hoped to pop it into her mouth before the dog realized what was happening. Using her thumb and index finger, she pushed the pill under the flew and into the cheek. Within a second, Tuppy spat it onto the floor. Julia tried again, determined to hold Tuppy's mouth shut. Tuppy was quicker. Altering her tactics, Julie picked up the slightly softened pill and coaxed it as far down the back of Tuppy's tongue as she dared. This time it disappeared, leaving Julia with a mild feeling of satisfaction. Seconds later, Tuppence vomited a small quantity of saliva, bile and a partially dissolved pill. Julia sighed heavily, cleaned up the mess and said, "Okay. On to plan C."

She took another pill from the blister pack, crushed it between two spoons and added the powdery result to a quarter cup of water. Filling the syringe as instructed, she propped it on a plate and settled Tuppence her lap. What she hoped would be an easy squirt became the labour of Sisyphus—the solution went in and it dribbled out, it went in, it came out——over and over again. Finally, Julia reasoned that some of the solution was getting swallowed and before her patient lost all patience, she put the syringe in the sink and took Tuppy to the fenced backyard.

On shaky legs, the little dog managed to negotiate the short grass of spring, and only when she stopped to relieve herself did she require *Mom's* help to remain upright. "Good job, 2p," praised Julia, using the nickname she'd scorned when first coined by her brother. Jake had actually suggested the name Tuppence and Julia liked its uniqueness and the fun of saying Tuppy puppy. It was only a few years ago she learned Jake's suggestion was a reverse reference to the high cost of French bulldogs.

By bedtime, Julia hoped Tuppence was as tired as she was and she may have been, but this didn't prevent unsteady pacing for most of the night. They got through the next day having frequent naps, and though Julia tempted her with all her favourites, Tuppy refused to eat. They finally had a breakthrough when, after another syringe session, Tuppence tottered over to her bowl and successfully lapped up some water. Julia offered her chicken broth and she drank some of that too but she wouldn't even look at real food. Over the next couple of days, Julia alternated between hope and despair.

When they finally got into the clinic, the pragmatic Dr. Shaw expressed grave concerns regarding Tuppy's refusal to eat. He mentioned her old age and raised the possibility that, though extremely rare, the dog may have suffered a stroke. "There are times when the best decision is to say goodbye."

Feeling like a threadbare rag doll, Julia fought to control her emotions. "Are you talking about euthanasia?"

His nod was almost imperceptible but his words were clear. "Death by starvation is not a good option."

Julia straightened her spine and squared her shoulders. "Tuppence will eat today."

"And if she doesn't?"

Julia stood firm. "She will."

By the time they got home, Julia had worked out a plan. Keeping an eye on Tuppy, she made a dinner of chicken, rice and carrots, and put some of it into the blender with a little water. When it was the consistency of thick soup, she poured it into a bowl.

Placing the bowl next to Tuppy, Julia said, "If you can drink water, you can drink food." The dog stared into the bowl but made no attempt to eat. Julia dipped her index finger into the purée and held it under Tuppy's nose. Tuppy turned away. Julia dapped some on her muzzle. Tuppy turned again, this time wiping her face across Julia's sleeve.

"All right, Miss Tuppence, if you won't come to the food, the food is coming to you." She picked up the bowl, set it on the table and retrieved her turkey baster from the oven drawer. Lifting Tuppy to her lap and restraining her in the crux of her left elbow, Julia filled the turkey baster and before the dog could turn away, squeezed chicken purée into her mouth. Tuppy swallowed it all. Julia gave her more and Tuppy swallowed again. Soon she was opening her mouth and eating with obvious enthusiasm. Julia stared into Tuppy's deep brown eyes. They stared back, steady and focused and in that moment, Julia knew, at least for now, Tuppy intended to stay.

Felicity Sidnell Reid

THE RETURN OF BIRDS

Are the doves discussing the weather
as they strut up and down the deck rail?
Or are they designing a love nest
to hold a pair of white eggs in spring?
Coos pledge a life-time of loving.

Robins have checked out the crab apples
and scattered to hunt with their mates.
They stalk the twigs dropped by winter,
prise grass for a home on the rafters
they're planning to renovate.

The geese honk their message abroad
as they drift down to glean a field.
They've raised grown goslings close by
and now they're retaking possession—
whatever the future may bring.

Wally Keeler

THE POLITICS OF SPRING

In spring
the snow disperses
like a mob of resentful rioters.
There are wounds waking in white fields
where grass grows green – an opening eye.
In spring the snow goes a. w. o. l.
In spring the sun leads a successful guerrilla movement or coup d'etat.
In spring there is an insurrection of grass, flower and love.
All winter wild our flesh forgot the sedition of sunlight.

No one votes spring into power.
Is spring a colonizer force?
Are robins infiltrated foreign agents
sabotaging snowmobile trails,
encouraging Green Power?
Spring is a state of growth that enables multicolourfulism.
(Winter is a onecolour regime).
The sun prosecutes and executes snow vigorously.
The sun dictates; ignores all appeals.
April showers are tears wrung from winter thawing on the gallows of
warmth.
Summer is the sun's gift of appeasement
for the coercive force to eliminate snow.

Fall is a word that speaks for itself.

If a poet were the premier of something,
what might that something be?
Would it be a nation of slavish poetry lovers?
Would the national militia consist of mighty tulips armed with colour
and solarshine?
Would the national anthem be a long joyful sigh after love?
Would the Union of Pollen Producers go on strike
demanding higher rates of sunlight
and more elaborate fringe benefits
such as lighter showers
and heavier dew?
Would the Creative Intelligence Agency report
that the Insect Pollen Transportation Organization had been infiltrated
by dissident outside agitators, such as breezes?

Then what would our foreign policy be?
Would we accept only immigrants carrying passport dreams?
Then what about the refugees from Grief and defectors from Despair?
Would we send out ambassadors to collect the neglected?
Would we establish dipoematic relations with Pain,
negotiate for a ceasefire
and settle for shorter durations?

Will we pick and choose our enemies
at the drop of a poem
and, once again, come charging,
singing our glorious anthem,
the Battle Hymn of the Poetic?

mia burrus

MARCH 20 2022, THE TORONTO ZEN CENTRE

The city garden already shelters snowdrops. The traffic noise is embroidered by robin song. We are now *in camera* instead of on camera: there is nowhere to hide. Though distanced, we are always aware of each other—a flash of robe, an unintended sigh, one's silent struggle, another's silent strength. The bell, block, moktok, and gong sound modulated and musical. The days, tightly set, unwind in peace. Behind closed doors, the cooks prepare their offerings. In gratitude we square dance in and out of countless rooms with rags and brooms. We align our minds: Roshi is magnetic north.

> kitchen shoes!
> dinner gong's soft tones
> follow my steps

Ronald Mackay

IN SWEET REJOICING

"In Sweet Rejoicing" was inspired by my friend John Reid Young's short story, "Illegal Immigrant," in his collection, A Shark in the Bath and Other Stories: Tenerife Tales Book 2. *John's family, of Scottish and English origin, have lived in Tenerife for over 200 years.*

The statue stands on a rock outside the village of Garachico overlooking the grey Atlantic. A man in vigorous mid-stride, his gaze on the distant Americas. A suitcase clutched in his left hand. A hole in place of his heart.

"That's the Emigrant." John pointed. "He represents all those many Tinerfeños who have left our islands for the New World."

John lit his pipe and told me this story.

***

On his twelfth birthday, Toño started in the banana plantation belonging to the Count, working alongside his father. It's what boys did, then. From the terraces on the mountainside, Toño could enjoy the sights and sounds of his tiny village: the fishermen rowing home; the comforting sounds of the carpenter's saw and the cobbler's hammer; the church bells that sanctified the day with prayer.

Everything changed the Christmas Toño turned 17. At Mass, he approached the Nativity, the better to see Baby Jesus, his eyes smiling and his arms open as he lay in his manger. And that's when Toño first saw an angel! Her name was Eva, the youngest daughter of Fausto the shoemaker. From that day on, Toño never missed Sunday Mass.

After Mass, young men and women, fresh in Sunday clothes, would stroll in groups around the plaza. They might exchange a few shy words, one with another. In those days, that's how courting began, how marriage came about.

Toño and Eva were content with these modest conversations. But not Fausto. He wanted more for his only daughter than a life of drudgery married to a plantation worker. So before Toño and Eva could even get to know each other, Fausto spoke to Toño.

"Your shoes are worn, Toño. I will repair them, without charge, because I like the look of you."

As he re-soled the shoes, Fausto asked, "What will you do with your life, Toño?"

"Exactly what I do now. Enjoy village life, the rhythm of the seasons, my work in the Count's plantation." And because Fausto said nothing, Toño felt obliged to add, "I may become foreman when my father retires."

"In the Americas, a man prospers and becomes rich." Fausto winked at Toño. "Then, he can return and marry the girl of his choice."

Toño heard these as words of encouragement. The wily Fausto, however, knew that once seduced by the Americas, men seldom returned.

"But I have no money for the passage!" Toño felt inadequate.

"Who needs money?" Fausto winked again. "I have connections."

And that was how Toño secured the promise of a passage to Venezuela, even though emigration was illegal in those days and only undertaken in secret.

Eva tried to dissuade Toño. But since they were not engaged—Fausto had acted before promises could be made—their conversations were oblique and public.

Eva would feign brightness. "Who in our village is not happy with the work they have and the church they worship in? Our love for home is as natural as breathing."

Confused, Toño could only repeat what Fausto had hinted at: "But things can be different."

"Different?" Eva shook her head. "We love our traditions, and what we love, don't we want to embrace forever?"

"The Americas offer opportunities." Again, Toño echoed Fausto. He paused and looked longingly at Eva, trying to make her understand what he felt in his heart. "I will return in two years. Three at most," he said softly.

During Christmas Mass, just as Father Francisco announced the triumphant words, *For unto you is born this day a Saviour,* a stranger touched Toño's elbow. Toño followed him in silence. From Fausto's workshop, he collected the cardboard suitcase, left there in readiness for this very secret occasion. On reaching the rock above the harbour, Toño turned and looked back. Eva stood at the church door, lit candles bright behind her. She opened her arms. The wordless gesture told Toño that Eva loved him and would wait for his return. From the portico, Eva watched Toño pause, his hand on his heart. Then, as he removed his hand, the setting sun passed clean through him. Eva blinked—and Toño was gone.

Soon after, wily old Fausto sprang into action. He encouraged suitable men to woo his daughter, but though many suitors came, she showed no interest. Eva was steadfast. But Fausto persisted. In those days, a woman was expected to marry young, have children, see them marry, and welcome grandchildren.

In Venezuela, life was hard. First, Toño had to pay off the cost of his passage. He cut sugar cane and harvested cocoa, working and saving, clinging to the memory of Eva, his family and his beloved village. Alone on his first Christmas, he attended Mass in Maracaibo's cathedral. In the flickering shade, the priest proclaimed, *For unto you is born a Saviour, which is Christ the Lord.* Those joyful words filled Toño with memories.

The memories drove him to work the harder. He bought a truck and drove it tirelessly between Caracas and the oil refineries of Maracaibo.

The following Christmas, instead of returning home, he bought a second truck, recalling Fausto's urging to return rich.

Back in Garachico, Fausto continued to pressure Eva: "Once a man leaves, he forgets." Relentlessly he sowed doubt in Eva's mind just as he had sown ambition in Toño's.

By his third Christmas in Venezuela, Toño owned five trucks. He made plans to return to his village and to Eva, but at the very last moment, he bought a sixth truck instead.

Fausto's persistence was beginning to pay off. Eva believed that a woman's life was to marry, have children, and welcome grandchildren. Discouraged by Toño's growing delays and hounded by her father, she submitted to his wishes. Eva married and welcomed her first child. Old Fausto made sure that Toño learned that this was so.

To overcome his disappointment and what he told himself was Eva's betrayal, Toño worked even harder, although he no longer knew why. His life had lost its meaning. More years passed. His fleet prospered and grew.

Eva welcomed two more children into her small world before her husband died. She grew older, stouter, happy enough with her children, and then with her grandchildren. But there were evenings, standing in the portico of the church after Mass, when she could still close her eyes and see Toño as she had seen him on that final Christmas, his arm extended, the setting sun piercing his heart. And hers.

Toño was tiring of his trucks, of his solitary life in an alien country. He cherished bittersweet memories of home, of loss and sadness. His life was no longer supported by a purpose.

On Christmas Eve, as was his custom, Toño attended Mass in Maracaibo's great cathedral. Listening to the bells tolling in the shadows of the tower and the priest proclaiming the miracle of Christ's birth, Toño could no longer hold back the tears of grief from all those years of hardship, exile, betrayal and disappointment. Toño wept.

Suddenly, through his silent tears, he saw Eva smiling at him across the manger. Bewildered, he reached for her but before he could grasp her, she was swallowed by the crowd of worshippers. Frantic, he was swept into the plaza, but Eva had vanished. Toño stood desolate and forsaken.

"Don Antonio!" Father Roberto called, gently taking his arm. "Come!" Toño followed Father Roberto into the sacristy where the old priest sat him down.

"You appear in need, my son."

"I am, Father."

"What is your need?"

"I need my home," Toño answered simply. "I need those I left behind in Garachico."

"Tenerife?" Father Roberto too was from the Canary Islands.

"My father and my mother lived in that village all their lives. Their ancestors too. I need to return, Father. That village is my home. It is where I left all that I truly loved."

In the shaded alcoves of prayer-lapped stone, where the fragrance of centuries lingers and the eternity of God's love dwells forever, Toño poured out his heart; and because he understood, Father Roberto listened. Toño told his story from the very beginning: of Eva; their walks in the plaza after Mass; their unspoken promises one to the other. How Eva had left him. Or was it, perhaps, that he had abandoned her? Father Roberto listened until Toño had finished all that he had to say, all that he had never spoken of before to anyone. Toño shed the tears of a lifetime.

Then, in the silent candlelight, Father Roberto spoke.

"The principal tragedy of life, my son, lies in the many ways we trespass upon one other. This is why we must learn to forgive. Regret is robbing you of your present and your future, both. Your life halted at the moment of injury. That wound is causing you to drown in deepest pain."

Toño bowed his head. He knew this to be true.

"You must forgive Eva," said the priest.

Perplexed, Toño raised his eyes. "Father, I *have* forgiven Eva. Long ago, she asked for my mercy, and I gave it." He turned his tormented eyes to the priest. "It is myself I cannot forgive, Father."

Understanding Toño's self-imposed suffering, Father Roberto spoke quietly. "Just as you learned to forgive Eva, you can learn to forgive yourself, Don Antonio."

"But success intoxicated me, Father. I failed Eva. My failure to return as promised is unforgivable."

Father Roberto put his hand on Toño's. "It is the unforgivable that we must strive to truly forgive."

Toño looked at the older man, puzzled.

"Torment robs you of everything. Each of you broke an unspoken promise, but such trespasses do not condemn you to live pointless lives. You forgave Eva. Eva accepted your forgiveness and renewed her life. You must now forgive yourself and repair yours."

"How, Father? How can I forgive my broken promise?"

"Forgiveness, my son, is not the forgiveness of an act, but it lies in offering forgiveness to the person who acted wrongly. Forgiveness becomes an act of love when it is aimed at a person. You forgave Eva as she forgave you, as two people, one to the other. In the same way you can forgive yourself. We cannot undo the past, but we must not allow it to destroy the present."

As the two old Canary Islanders talked, Toño grew in understanding. He learned that all lives endure suffering in the face of regret; that the act of self-forgiveness would free him from his trespass and allow him to regain a love for his own person; that it may never be too late to fulfill a sacred promise.

In the darkness, the two men prayed together. Two simple men who loved their villages and the people among whom they had been born and nurtured.

Home at last, Toño dismissed the taxi before it reached his village. He felt a need to stand alone on the very spot facing the ocean from which, those long years ago, he had left in secret, promising wordlessly to return.

He smelled the salty Atlantic across which he had twice travelled and began to feel once more the sweet sense of belonging. The church doors lay open. Eva stood there smiling, the candles bright behind her. She stretched out her arms to him and he to her.

Grey-haired, creased and bowed by the years, they touched. All of time and both their lives were consummated in that very moment.

Toño and Eva, arm in arm, walked into their church. At one with each other, together at last, they listened to the priest. *Thanks be to God who gives us victory through the birth of the Lord Jesus Christ.* In the manger, the Baby Jesus smiled and opened his arms to embrace them both in grace and truth, knowing everything there was to know about each of them.

***

Having finished his story, Juan refilled his pipe. Neither of us spoke. Our silence was broken by the peal of church bells.

Come, give thanks! Christmas is a festival of gratitude, a time to offer thanks to God whose Son guides us through life, brings us consolation in times of darkness, and joy everlasting.

Reva Nelson

BREATHING IN LIGHT

In and out
Inspire alas expired
Through the storm
Swirling frost
Takes its bite

Snow shards
Sting my eyes, stab my heart
I don't have you to call
You're not there
You lost your fight

There is no sharing of victories
Big or small
No glass of wine
On winter's balcony
In soft twilight

No trips anticipated
No laughs in snuggles
Nor being annoyed
By your chain saw snores
In the calm of night

Snow melts my cold heart
Yet still, buds appear, birds chirrup
Daffodil shoots poke out
Anticipating sunshine
And bright yellow light

Ted Amsden

MONKS COVE, COBOURG

I go to the lake to listen
knowing I have never heard a wave I understood

and I have listened hard
followed from right to left and back again
sought in curl and slope for syllable and intonation
noted slapping slinking scurrying rushing tumbling
                    roaring and more

I have no idea what is being said
it is why I return

full of sound and some days fury
likely signifying something
but nothing I need to worry about

John Unruh

WOODSMOKE

Harry was hard to get along with. There really wasn't much more to say. He left the impression he would be on almost everyone he met, and generally fulfilled the expectation in anybody who had the misfortune of meeting him again.

And he knew the nurses would agree. He could feel them watching behind his back, sharing looks as he sat by the bed, holding her hand while she slept, because regular visiting hours were over and he shouldn't have been there. But he'd arrived anyway and didn't leave when they asked. He'd nodded his head instead, mumbled an excuse, and sat down.

The awkward, strange little man.

People were always amazed that a woman like Beth ever conceded to marry him. And truth be told, he'd been amazed too. He'd always considered himself lucky that way. Lucky in love, if nothing else. Lucky to have met her.

***

Beth hadn't been a captive audience either, the summer they met. She'd been hired to organize the kitchen at Kylie's lodge and emerged that first day from the floatplane with the two chambermaids, Marta and Sheila. All three stepped onto the dock, one after the other, fresh-faced and full of virtue. It was the start of the season, so the guides hadn't arrived yet and the camp was otherwise empty; but there would be an abundance of men around in a week, with a new batch every week for the season. It was the same way every year. And the ladies that came to fill these roles never wanted for attention.

That particular summer, Sheila took the brunt of it, easily the prettiest. The guests described her as vivacious, in the way people did at the time. She was a self-professed activist who eventually became involved with one of the founding members of Greenpeace. As far as Harry knew, she still worked with the organization's latest iteration. Beth still received regular postcards, even now, full of passion and commentary, though as far as he knew she'd never responded to one of them.

Marta was a little different. Plain looking in comparison, but vibrant and full of good humour. She'd also proved herself a first-rate storyteller right off the mark, and that made her popular. After the one summer at Kylie's, she moved to New Zealand, became a postie and never bothered to marry. She spent her life tripping around the world instead, whenever she could manage it. She and Beth had liked each other from the start and remained close throughout their lives. They'd talked endlessly on the phone on birthdays, and even managed a few visits despite the distance.

And then there was Beth. What could he say about Beth? He'd always seen her as a handsome woman. Quiet. Competent. Sincere. But what he loved most about her was her laugh. It was a full and easy laugh. The kind that never second-guessed itself. The kind of laugh that knew exactly when it would be needed, as though it had already incubated to full maturity before it was released. It was the kind of laugh that filled everything it touched.

And it was the first part of Beth that ever touched him, spilling from the floatplane just before she stepped onto the dock at Kylie's Lodge that first day—a reaction to something one of the other ladies had said. Or the pilot. Harry didn't know. He'd never thought to ask, even after all these years.

All he knew was that her laughter had been a gift to him. There was really no other way to put it.

***

When Kylie greeted the ladies that first day, Harry strode by them all to help the pilot unload the plane, not daring to look and see which one of the women owned that beautiful laugh. And it was this action that marked him. He felt all of their eyes tracing his back as he bent to his work, wondering at his silence and the lack of acknowledgement. In response, Kylie called him over, not thinking, because he knew Harry and he knew better than to do that, but he was so taken with the three ladies.

A small mountain of dread bloomed in Harry's gut and caused his diaphragm to lift into his lungs so he couldn't breathe or talk. But he stopped dutifully and did as he was asked. Names were exchanged. Hands were shaken. He smiled and forced himself to make eye contact. He even sustained it for a moment with Beth when she shook his hand and a gentle laugh emerged and he knew she was the one.

That was when Kylie felt encouraged. When he saw that look in Harry's eye. That moment of interest. He responded by complimenting Harry on his many years of service. He told the ladies that Harry managed the camp's maintenance single-handed and described him as indispensable.

All eyes turned to him then and Kylie knew right away he'd made a mistake. The silence that followed held the same effect as a clap of thunder. Harry went wide-eyed and mute. He sucked in a mouthful of air, packed it into his cramped lungs, and managed to excuse himself with a hiccup of words that conveyed something about a fire that needed starting.

As he walked away, Harry heard Kylie explain in apologetic tones that the fire was an evening tradition down by the lake, and that Harry wasn't much of a talker.

And, of course, he wasn't.

But unknown to Harry, that short exchange had singled him out in a way he would never have expected. From that point on, neither Sheila nor Marta managed to be overly polite to him. In fact, they found him increasingly odd and disagreeable as time went on. But Beth? She proved different. She'd seen something in him that she recognized. And the very thing that turned the others away stirred something deep within her.

***

As the season wore on, Harry's relationship with Beth grew out of the circumstances that surrounded them.

Most of the men that used Kylie's camp were different than Harry. In general, they were loud and boisterous men—drinkers and talkers and men on vacation. They spent their time at the lodge working to subdue the wilderness that surrounded them and wrench life from it. Many were there to make their presence known—to catch the big fish and take it home. And to Harry they represented a small but growing scar on the landscape. They didn't love the land like he did. They just didn't. Not in the same way.

Despite this, he made no issue with any of them, and they showed no malice in return. They were part of the picture and had as much of a right to it as anyone. And Harry was fully aware he couldn't have one without the other.

Beth, on the other hand, couldn't bring herself to see it the same way. She held many of the same convictions Harry did, about the land and their place in it, but unlike Harry she voiced her feelings when the need rose inside and she was avoided for this. Her dislike of most of the men and what they represented was too plainly worn. And her days were often a trial of sideways comments and jokes.

Harry saw it all happening of course. He was tuned to this kind of thing and always had been, and he offered only kindness in return. In this way, they began to exchange smiles and nods of encouragement and secret looks. Then, in the evenings, Beth began to linger by the fire with Harry after the others left for the relative warmth of the lodge. Most nights they just sat saying little or nothing. They listened to the land, and the fire. They watched the woodsmoke drift by and the embers as they died against the twilight's final fade.

Beth tried to explain it all to Marta at the wedding. She told her friend that Harry had a kind of tenderness. It might be hard to see, but he had it. And it spoke to her. Marta could only say that it must be true, considering the present circumstances, and she wished the best for her friend. She wished the best for Harry too.

It was all she could do.

***

But now, so many years later, it didn't really matter what people thought. A lifetime of love and labour and accomplishment had amounted to little more than a morning mist. Her mind had left her, dying back as softly as those very same embers so long ago. All the memories. The love they'd shared. Everything. It had all drifted away until Harry found he'd been made into a stranger. To her. To the world. Even to himself.

And yet, he couldn't make himself let it all go. Not yet.

He listened to the nurses until their hushed whispers left him, as he knew they would—one off to his rounds, the other to her coffee.

He didn't waste a moment then. Everything was ready and this was the only chance he'd get. He stood up and left the room to retrieve the wheelchair by the nurses' station and returned to position it beside the bed.

He had no choice but to rouse Beth then. He bent over the bed to remove the blanket and sheet that covered her. She murmured through a haze of medication as he slipped his arms beneath her and lifted.

The moment surprised him and his breath hitched in his throat. She came up easily, almost without effort. One disease had taken her mind and everything they'd come to treasure together. The other, the one that finally forced her into hospital, had consumed her. He had to stand with her for a moment by the bed to steady himself. He breathed. She folded into him. Instinct perhaps. Or muscle memory. It didn't matter. The effect was the same. His heart quaked.

When he felt able, he turned around, placed her in the chair and covered her again. They moved through the empty hall together and into the elevator, two flights down, out the big double doors—not a soul around. Nobody that cared, at least. A few seconds later they were by the car. He opened the door carefully and set her inside.

He had pillows stacked up high on the centre seat and he leaned her against them. He smoothed her hair back out of the way so her cheek could feel the cool freshness of the linen, just the way she liked. He covered her in an old shawl, one she'd knit herself. It didn't seem so impossibly long ago that her hands had worked the yarn—strong and determined. He wrapped it now around her shoulders, tucking it in tight to surround her diminished frame, and placed the hospital blanket on top.

Then he drove. For the better part of an hour, they moved past endless fields where ripening wheat glowed dully in the moon's silvery light. Eventually, the fields turned to pasture and scrubland. And then the forest emerged, stretching a line of shadow up from the ground and into the night sky like the edge of a torn off page. He continued to drive through the forest, each breath and every beat of his heart bringing them closer until, finally, they arrived.

He pulled onto the property and followed tracks of dirt and stone and gravel toward the lake. He stopped the car and stared through the windshield at the faint outline of the cabin's roof where it interrupted the treeline.

"We're here, Beth," he said, his voice hoarse from lack of use. He cleared it. "Just like we planned."

She stirred but was still too heavily sedated to wake. Harry got out of the car and walked around the back to reach Beth's side. He opened the door and slipped his arms beneath her to lift. She felt heavier this time. He was tired from the drive, but filled with purpose, and he rallied his strength. He carried her up the walk. He stood with her in front of the little cabin and gazed longingly at it.

He'd built it with his own hands. Every timber. Every fitting and function. And as he stared at it with Beth in his arms, he recognized the power of it. Maybe for the first time. He understood the work, and how it kept him going. The need to finish what he'd started.

He wanted so desperately to take her in and show it to her. To have her exclaim her delight and her joy and give her approval to every detail.

He wanted her to sit down with him at the kitchen table and talk to him about all the wonderful things they were going to do, and how lovely it would all be.

Then he looked down at her face, serene in the shadowy half-light offered by the moon, and his heart heaved.

They'd stood there only once together, when they first bought the land nearly a decade ago, and dreamed. They'd planned to spend their final years there in peace, far away from the world and its troubles.

They'd promised to grow old together.

He turned, forcing himself on, and carried her to a path that led down beside the cabin to a short strip of beach. He was careful with his footing in the dark. He'd learned the position of every stone and every root on the property, but his cargo was precious and his mind threatened at every turn to retreat into memory and leave him stranded.

When he neared the waterfront, he moved off the path toward a dark, low bench. He set Beth down on it and laid her gently on her side. There were more pillows there. She murmured in her sleep and nuzzled the linen, adjusting her cheek against it. He stayed with her until she drifted off again. Then he moved to the fire he'd prepared earlier that day.

He pulled a single match from his pocket and sparked it to life with the edge of his nail. He reached down and held it close to the shavings where they lay just below the kindling. The fire sprang up quickly and soon began to breathe, feeding on darkness and chill air to spread its warmth.

He stayed with it for a time, watched the flame lick into the wood, and let it grow to a healthy size before backing away. Then he moved to the bench and lifted the pillow where Beth's head rested. He moved the extra pillows to the side and positioned himself where the pillows had been. Without a thought, his hand moved down to brush against her cheek, and then back to her fine silvery-white hair. He began to stroke it, moving his hand in a familiar pattern, from her brow to the top of her ear and over again. His gaze fixed on the dancing flames and he lost track of time. Occasionally, the breeze coming over the lake turned and the smoke curled past him—the sweet smell of woodsmoke, filling his lungs.

He breathed it in.

When the last flame flickered and died and the embers began to cool, he took a long, slow breath and let it out.

It was over now. All that remained was a soft fleeting glow, half buried in ash, and the darkness all around. Beth's breath rose and fell in a steady rhythm. She was comfortable, but she needed more than he could offer.

He leaned down and kissed her cheek. For one long moment he drew her into him—her sweet scent, the familiar feel of her. Then, with great effort, he stood and lifted her again. He carried her carefully back to the car.

They'd have missed her by now.

Diane Taylor

THIS FERTILE MOMENT

There's a big hole in my heart. Joanna left home in September for university in Guelph, leaving me with her empty room. Nothing, nothing happens in there. It's dead space. She came home at Christmas and it was like an oasis had suddenly sprung forth from the barren sands. Her laughter over my silly jokes and the clatter of her new heels on our hardwood floors; her excitement about her profs and her unbounded enthusiasm for the archaeology dig she had signed up for in the south of France—a place called Rennes le Château.

Did I know, she thrilled, her thick brown hair swirling about her shoulders, that Mary Magdalene probably had three children, the first— they think—by John the Baptist, and the other two by Jesus? And that Mary may have written about her life with him and hidden the scrolls near this chateau? To myself, I marvel over these interests of hers, especially since we were never a religious family. She hugged me, too. This was new. As a family, we hadn't hugged, but now this familiar daughter was bringing unfamiliar ways into my world. Actually, I had to admit I liked the physicality of the hugs.

Archaeology was her major, and by some quirk of curriculum, Joanna had finagled a dance minor. She was off to an exchange conference next year in Havana and could hardly wait to see Cuban ballet and meet the dancers. Suddenly my home-grown girl was a young woman of global dimensions. It was too soon, too fast. Earth was whirling into space without me.

When both my kids were in public school, the only travel I'd had time, money or inclination for was a weeklong visit with my sister Sue in Miami. She was eight months pregnant, and at forty it felt like a miracle.

This baby would be like a rebirth after the devastating loss Sue and her husband Marc had suffered during Hurricane Andrew. They'd spent that whole night in the shower stall while wind roared and water rose around their ankles. In the morning, when they crawled out from the rubble, everything was gone—the barn, all the trees, neighbours' ranch houses, telephone poles. The yearling Sue had bottle fed because the mother had no milk had been killed by flying metal roofing. I can still hear her sobbing when she called to tell me.

Now as I drive to meet Sue at the Tim Hortons in Stouffville, I remember the day she met me at the airport. I barely recognized this woman. She looked big enough to be having twins, maybe even triplets, but she was beautiful—the epitome of health—tanned, with her sun-bleached hair almost waist length. The next day we went to the waterfront park and spread out a blanket. As she lay on her side, she was like a reclining madonna, full and ready for this birth.

That was five years ago. Her labour was long, there were complications and the baby was stillborn. Internal damage meant there would be no more. Their marriage broke up. I wept for her. And now she's come home, I feel that more is being asked of me than I can give.

We meet in the restaurant, pick up coffee and doughnuts, pick out a table.

"Sarah, that's a great turtleneck," she says about my new purchase.

"Thanks, I was pretty pleased with it. On sale," I say.

"I applied for a job at the hospital," she says.

"Yeah?"

"But they said my experience is not recent enough."

"Oh, too bad." I try to hide my own disappointment.

"Well, my unemployment has come through, so I'm fine."

Unemployment. How has it come to this? The woman has two degrees, for crissake—one in nursing, the other in photography. I want to stop worrying about her. I have enough worries of my own. "That's good," I say.

She stirs her coffee. She seems tense. I know she is trying to look as if everything's fine, but I know her too well; I'm her sister. But I'm not capable of being her social worker. Actually, I need someone to support me. I haven't told her about Joanna's empty room, all the soccer games I go to even though I don't really care about soccer (although god knows I want Jonathon to score as many goals as he does), or that Chuck is unhappy with the amount of time I spend at the school of music. These all seem trivial to what Sue is facing, and yet they're my life.

"How does Joanna like university?"

"She loves it. Really excited about her courses. Who'd have thought that a child of mine would sign up for an archaeological dig in the south of France looking for hidden scrolls that may or may not exist?"

"It's amazing!"

"You know what her favourite mantra is now?"

"No, what?" Sue asks.

"All shall be well."

"Hmm," she says. "I used to think like that …"

Her voice drifts, and I share what Joanna has told me about how the church maligned Mary Magdalene for two millennia, casting her as a prostitute when current research shows she was possibly the wife of Jesus. Sue wonders what research might unearth in another fifty or a hundred years. But she doesn't ask what it's like not knowing where my daughter has gone. She does ask my plans for her room and I'm afraid she's hoping I'll take her in. But Chuck and I just can't afford it. And how would it change our relationship as sisters?

And it's not really an empty room. Joanna is there even if she isn't. Her life-size poster of Baryshnikov leaps on the wall, her frilly pink Grade Eight graduation dress still hangs in the closet, her first camera is on the top shelf of the bookcase, and, and . . . I am suddenly overwhelmed with the magnitude of the lost gems of her past that are my past, too, and my own inability to accept barren rooms that had once been fertile. I too feel like an archaeologist, and I don't like being forced into this role.

Sue looks at me as if waiting for an offer. I return her look. "Sue, I can't help you, I'm of no use to you." What I mean is that I can't carry her burdens as well as my own, but that sounds too selfish. And I can't admit that all was not well.

She gathers her thoughts. "I know, Sarah. I'm sorry."

It's over. We get up, walk to our cars. No bye, no hug.

Back home, I pour myself a gin and tonic and sit on the porch, where I know the sun will reach past the shade of the still nude branches of the maple tree. I let my whole body fall forward from the waist so that my head is resting between my knees, feel the blood rush to nourish my brain and face, feel my whole back and neck relax, and stay like that for a full minute. Slowly, I bring my body back upright and as usual am amazed at how this simple action empties my mind. You can't be worried if you're not thinking! I sip my drink. Smile into the April sun.

Two weeks zoom past. We have some of Joanna's friends from school here for a few days while they party and make lists of the things they will need on the dig. At the top of the list is a bottle of Niagara ice wine. Crazy to my mind, but it's a must, they say, to bring something uniquely Canadian. Jonathon went to the hospital for tests because he had a dizzy spell at soccer practice. All they found was very low haemoglobin. What does this mean? More tests. I try to keep calm.

Sue calls to say a photo shop is interested in her résumé and is offering part-time, but it could be full-time if she were to get some current experience.

"Great!" I say, truly relieved. "Something's bound to come up."

"How are the kids?" she asks.

So I tell her about Jonathon. "He has low haemoglobin and is dizzy and sleepy lately. Do you have any idea what this could be?" My heart is thudding.

She's quiet for a few seconds, then her professional voice says that it could be something as simple as low iron. Of course she would never say it could be a brain tumour. Still, I feel better.

Another two weeks zoom past. It *is* low iron with Jonathon, and he's on ferrous sulphate for a while. He's safe and I can stop worrying on that front. Joanna leaves soon for Rennes le Château. She's overjoyed with my gift of a bottle of ice wine.

The phone rings one morning. It's Joanna asking if Aunt Sue has found a job yet. I tell her what Sue told me. "Well," says Joanna, in this new way she has that everything works out, that everyone is a piece in the puzzle, "our director is looking for a photographer for the dig."

Incredible! But what are the chances Sue would want to globetrot for experience? We hang up, I call Sue.

Early June, early afternoon, and Sue has come for a quick visit before I head over to the school of music.

"Perrier?" I keep it on hand for Sue because it's part of her current clean-up-her-act regimen. I make myself a gin and tonic.

We move out to the porch, and the sun splashes onto our bare legs, bare feet. The mood is light, but she tells me she's lonely. That she misses places and people (and horses are people for Sue) from her former life. This is the most she has ever said about her troubles. I think that for her, the past is not dead, may never pass into the past. This is who she is—my sister, with all she has lived through, and all she hasn't.

Then it hits me that I, too, have a past with things that I miss—she and I are not really all that different. She has tough stuff to deal with, and so do I. Our "stuff" may be different, but we both have it. I am both scandalized and pleased with this revolutionary insight.

I take a deep breath, knowing that any word could be the wrong word. We sip our drinks, watch a multitude of new frothy green-gold maple leaves unfurl above us. This unstoppable softening of the world needs no words to reach into us as we sit there in silence.

When we were kids, we called each other Kiddo.

"Say, Kiddo," I feel a smile bubbling up inside me, "have you thought about the dig in France? Do you think it will be the kind of experience you'd like?"

Words rush out. "I do, oh I do. I want to grab this and run with it. I told the shop owner, and he's excited, too."

"Then it's perfect for you. I'm so glad."

"And I'd be there to look out for Joanna."

"It's working out," I say, amazed.

Then we just sit in silence in the fine company of the unfurling green-gold maple leaves. No thought, no archaeology, no past, no future, just this unencumbered fertile moment.

All shall be well? Could be.

Kathryn MacDonald

SING PRAISES

Sing like songbirds in the meadow
their voices lifting among weeds and wildflowers,
light as a chorus of flutes. And you
happy for blossoms – blue   yellow   white
and the pale green tinge of Queen Anne's Lace –
for grasses   swaying plumes of seeds.

Praise the song and hidden singers.
Praise the solitary yellow-bellied sapsucker.
Praise the fourteen blackbirds perched on the fence.
Praise the little ship tied in her slip.

Gwynn Scheltema
GRIGGLES

The yellow grass is flat under the apple tree. Perhaps
from the deer, or my burly brother busy picking
by the brimming bushel basket full
and carrying them to the barn,
where only the perfect garner
Father's pride and
those not quite whole
are tossed to the steaming cider pile.

Then in aprons red and white
Mother and my sisters slice
and dice for pies
and jams and jellies
litter the floor with curls
of rosy peels
discard the too-small morsels
to boil into maple-apple butter.

A ladder still
pokes fingers through the branches
but there are no good apples
left—
save one small griggle
high on a topmost limb,
small and gnarled
forgotten like this lame boy.

But I shall find a way
to climb
Jacob's ladder
and I shall choose
that apple—
for it grows closest to the sky.

Michael Croucher

DAPHNE'S CANON

Edward McGrath stepped back from the baby grand piano, folded the note as he'd found it, and slipped it into the envelope. The envelope smelled of lavender. He breathed deeply and savoured the fragrance. She'd always loved lavender. Her eyes seemed to watch him from her photo on the lid of the piano.

Daphne had played that piano often. Always beautifully. He'd found the envelope in the piano bench while searching for a CD of her favourite music. She must have known he'd find it there eventually.

He thought about what he'd just read in the note and shook his head. "No bloody thank you," he said aloud, but he still wanted the envelope and the note with him when he went to their special place. He tucked it into his shirt pocket. It was late afternoon on a beautiful autumn day. A perfect time to go.

He left the house by the side door and descended the hill. Halfway down, the view across the pond stopped him. The water reflected fall colours from the many stands of trees in High Park. Shimmering magically, the image was stunning. He admired it before resuming his pace. The view from their bench would also be glorious.

He and Daphne had favoured a park bench that was partly hidden in a thicket of trees and bushes at the north end of Grenadier Pond. From there they could see along the body of water and up its heavily treed eastern bank. They'd enjoyed sitting there, listening to the chatter of birds, the leaves rustling in the wind and the occasional splash of feeding fish.

Edward needed all of that. He needed it now. Since she'd gone, the bench had become his place to think. A sanctuary where he could come to terms with his grief and consider his future, now that retirement was to follow on the heels of his loss. The splendid setting should revive his spirits.

At a bay thick with bulrushes at the pond's north end, he crossed a short footbridge and arrived at the bench. Sheltered from the clutter of urban life and the buzz of Toronto traffic, he sat and watched the changing light. The evening sun was casting a fine orange glow. He sighed deeply. The stresses of his work day drifted away.

Edward mentally ticked off one more day. Only twenty-three to go. Then he could start and finish more days here. Lose himself in memories or plan visits to the families of his grown children or personal outings to art galleries and museums. Or . . . he could just sit and ponder.

He closed his eyes and let the solitude and the hush of the place embrace him. This was exactly what he wanted. At the point of dozing, he was disturbed by a distant clatter. A vaguely familiar sound. It moved towards him and grew louder.

He recognized the noise. It came from the path on the other side of the bulrushes. Yes . . . a bicycle, with a playing card or a sports card attached to its frame. The card snapped rapidly through the spokes—a mechanized staccato. Persistent. Irritating.

He opened one eye but couldn't see the offending cyclist. The noise came and went in waves. He stood, eager to admonish the culprit. Suddenly, the noise stopped, seemingly in front of him. All he heard was the rustle of leaves and the whispering breeze. But there was no bicycle. No rider. Confused, Edward stepped forward and looked in both directions along the path. Still nothing. Dreaming . . . *I must have fallen asleep*. But it was so real, so invasive. It couldn't have been a dream.

Chilled, he buttoned up his coat and moved towards the street, ready to start his way back up the hill to his house. As he neared the end of the path, he heard the sound again. It was distant now, moving back along the far edge of the pond. He stopped for a moment and listened to the sound until it faded into the night. He shook his head. Not a dream then. Strange

… very strange. A short way up the hill, he turned for another look. The path was blocked from his view by the trees along the road. But no more clatter. Perhaps the rider had gone home.

There was a woman standing on the little bridge, waving her scarf toward where Edward had last heard the sound. Could it be the rider's mother? Well, perhaps not the mother; a little too old. The grandmother then.

Inside his home, Edward slumped into a leather wingback chair by the stereo. He took Daphne's favourite CD, slid it into the player and closed his eyes. He pictured her at the piano, her fingers dancing over the keys, playing the first piano piece on the CD. It was *Canon in D*. She'd always played that tune beautifully. After all, she had the skill. Studied piano at the Ontario Conservatory and was a highly regarded amateur musician. Edward had never played, but he'd loved watching and listening to Daphne play.

Sleep came midway through the long piece. He dreamed of her then, smiling at him. He heard her voice. *Go on. It's all right, Edward. Go on.*

Awake and ready to call it a night, he climbed the stairs to their bedroom. He spoke forcefully as he entered the bedroom, as if she was there. "Never, Daphne! Never!"

He deeply missed her. Cried about her often. He wished she was there now, talking and laughing. They'd go downstairs. She'd play for a while. And then they'd both enjoy a Manhattan as dinner cooked.

Days later, after a business trip, Edward sat in his front room. The house was quiet. He was restless. Depressed. He left the house and went down the hill to the pond to shake off his doldrums. He walked the winding paths around it before approaching the bench.

When he finally crossed over the small bridge, he felt invigorated and eager to sit. But the bench was occupied by a woman. Disappointed, he was prepared to walk past and go home.

He stopped short. It was the lady from a few nights ago. The lady who'd waved to someone from the bridge.

She nodded and smiled. "Good morning."

"Yes, it is a good morning. And you've found a lovely spot to enjoy it." He decided against claiming any entitlement to the bench, although he could scarcely remember anyone else sitting there at this time of day.

"I've enjoyed it here for many years," she said.

"I've never seen you."

"It's my special place. I come here to catch whispers."

"Whispers?" He tilted his head.

"Yes. Little touches of comfort. They're so important to me. I really couldn't carry on without them."

He didn't question her statement. "I come here quite often myself. It's strange that I've never seen you before. Well . . . until the other night that is."

"The other night?"

"Yes, you were standing nearby. I think you were waiting for someone on a bicycle."

She stood. Shocked. "You know about that? How? That's not possible."

"I heard it. Just after I arrived here, the bike came with a card in the spokes. It made quite the racket. I thought it stopped in front of me, but I couldn't see a rider or a bike. I heard it again. Then I saw you waiting as I left."

She sat back on the bench, pale faced, shaken. "But, I'm the only . . ."

"Are you all right?" He moved forward slightly.

"It's my Jimmy. He's always here for me. No one else can see or hear him."

Edward sat at the far end of the bench. "I'm afraid I'm not following this, Mrs. um . . ."

"Rowe."

"I'm not following you, Mrs. Rowe."

"He drowned in this pond—forty-one years ago. My Jimmy, my little messenger, he finds me here, whispers, lets me know he's all right."

"Well, I only heard the bike, I didn't see him. It was really very puzzling."

"I hear him all the time. And I've seen him, but only twice. He whispers to me. No one else has ever heard him, not even my daughters, when they're here with me. I've never let on. But to know that you've heard him, that's very hard to understand."

She tightened her coat ready to leave, but turned to him. "Actually, I had a similar experience to yours just a while ago."

"How so?"

"Sitting right here, I heard music, beautiful piano music."

"That's not so unusual, Mrs. Rowe. There are lots of houses nearby. Quite a few pianos, believe me. Probably someone practising, or listening to a stereo."

"No, the sound was all around me. It was as though I were sitting on the piano bench with the player. An excellent pianist. Playing one of my favourite tunes."

"And what tune was that?"

"I absolutely love *Canon in D*. I have since I was a child. I could listen to it for hours."

Edward looked at the woman as if seeing her for the first time.

"My name is Edward, Edward McGrath." He held out his hand, tentatively.

She shook it lightly. "Barbara, Barbara Rowe."

They walked back to the street and looked in opposite directions along it. She turned back to him. "Perhaps we could meet sometime for a coffee, Edward."

"My wife passed not too long ago. I'm still trying to come to terms with it all."

"Yes. I understand. I'm a widow myself. Have been for many years. It takes a long time, but believe me, it gets better. It always helps to have someone to talk to. Especially someone who's been through the same thing. If you'd like, you can usually find me on Wednesday and Friday mornings around 10 o'clock at the Grenadier Restaurant. It's right here in High Park. Do you know the one?"

"Yes, I do. I'm retiring soon, in a couple of weeks actually. I'll try and drop by."

She tapped him gently on the wrist letting her fingers rest on his flesh for a moment.

"Please do, Edward."

He sighed warmly at her touch.

Neither of them heard the happy clatter of bike spokes from the path, or the excited tinkling of piano keys coming from the bulrushes playing Canon in D.

Daphne's Canon in D.

Karen Walker

THE NATURE OF STARTING OVER

Username: Butterfly

"Don't bug me," I tell my daughter.

Swatting my words aside, she signs me up and chooses my username: Butterfly.

Men in the late stages of life—antennae bent or missing, holes in wings and the elbows of their cardigans—flutter across the laptop.

"Try it, Mum."

I haven't dated for thirty-two years. What a strange new world. Unnatural.

I type "Hello." Buzz. Buzz. I'm swarmed like a porch light at night, as if I'm the last flower, the last nectar they'll ever find.

Too much. I log out and caterpillar to the couch, to cocoon and ponder who I'll become now.

***

Having Shed My Stripey Larval Pyjamas

I'm meeting William at The Milkweed Cafe in Warkworth in a little black dress and a new bra.

My daughter, hoping I'd fly again after divorce, chose him. His picture—posing in a tweed jacket in a meadow of fellow wildflowers, a country manor in the distance—oozed style. "A blooming gentleman! Perfect for you."

Her advice: Play hard to catch. Only tell him my username. Otherwise, he'll pin me as desperate.

The door opens, and there he is. Hmm. Shorter, maybe a bit wilted. Weedier and certainly greyer than in his profile.

Rooted to the floor, William fiddles with his purple-flowered tie. "Hello," he says. "Call me Bill."

Gulp. Flitting like the fritillary I am, I alight beside him. "I'm Daphne."

***

Parasteatoda tepidariorum, the Common House Spider

Bill wants to move in.

My daughter tries to squash that, asking why risk my lovely new wings in his sticky web.

"Can't you two just date?"

As in coffee once a week and dinner theatre at the Best Western on Thursday nights, antiquing and strolling. Nature walks if we feel up to it.

We do. We've been exploring each other's flora and fauna. Bill has a gentle touch. It's been a long time.

"He'll suck you dry."

Whine. Whine. She's a mosquito in my ear. I'll end up driving him to doctor appointments and cutting his meat and putting shoes on all those feet.

He has four pairs and, yeah, that'd be a chore. A burden. But, right now, they sure do tickle.

Susan Statham

COME BACK

"Katie, you have to come home now."

"Adam?"

"Yes. Come home. Now."

"Why? I just got here." Kate was used to the unreasonable demands of her big brother, but this was beyond the pale.

"I mean it, Katie. Tell your friend you'll go swimming another day."

It had been a hot thirty-minute walk to Emma's house, and Kate hadn't been there long enough to even get a drink of water. "Jeez, Adam. What's the problem? And how did you get this number?"

Kate thought Emma was teasing when she'd answered her home phone, put her hand over the mouthpiece and said, "This is weird. It's for you."

"You're kidding, right?" Kate had laughed and crossed her arms.

But Emma shook her head and shoved the phone toward her. Now she was stuck talking to Adam, if you can call listening to commands talking. He'd only arrived home a few days ago, having just finished his second year at university, and had spent most of his time ordering her around. And how often did she have to remind him to call her Kate? She was almost fourteen.

"Mom gave me the number. She told me to call you home," said Adam.

"Then the least you can do is tell me why I have to turn around and walk all the way back before we even got to do anything."

"Dad dropped dead at the hospital."

Kate heard what her brother said but she couldn't process it.

"Katie did you hear me? Remember this morning, Dad took me to the hospital to get this rash checked out. It was a long wait and when we were leaving …" Adam's voice cracked. He took a deep breath. "Dad collapsed before we got out the door."

Kate felt surreal. She was at her friend's and in her body listening to her brother talking, but she was also somewhere else—somewhere she'd never been. "Is he … is he … dead?" she heard herself ask.

"His heart stopped but the doctors are working on him, at least they were when I left the hospital. We're waiting for a call and Mom needs you to come home. Okay?"

"Okay." Feeling more robot than human, Kate picked up her beach bag and left Emma's house the same way she'd entered. Walking home always felt longer because it was all uphill. This time it was a journey to mirror how she suddenly saw her life. Without her daddy it would be like scaling a mountain.

He made her feel she could do anything. When she was very little, he used to throw her up in the air and catch her before she hit the ground. Her mother's voice, "John, stop, she might get hurt," was lost in her own squeals of delight. And then he would lie down on their manicured lawn, his knees bent, his arms extended while Katie waited in a runner's crouch a few feet in front of him. "Okay Katie, ready? One, two, three—go!" She ran, and when she reached him, both palms grabbed his knees, she flipped and he guided her over his head to land on her feet in the soft grass. Her father was the strongest man she knew.

Kate had watched medical shows on television—TV doctors saving their patients with electric shocks. Is that what they were doing to her father? Were they bringing him back? He had to come back. They had only been apart once before.

When Kate was five, the company her father worked for shut down. Her dad's father, Grandpa Joe, saw it as the perfect time for his son to move back and help run the family construction company. The problem was Adam.

He didn't want to move, and he especially didn't want to move until he finished Grade Eight. Kate was too young to understand the discussions, the anger and the bartering that went into the final decision. All she knew was that one day her daddy left for another city in another province and for the next four months she cried herself to sleep.

Kate was halfway up the hill and with each plodding step the heat radiating from the cement increased another degree. It had been a day like this the summer they visited Toronto, her mother's hometown. Granny had just moved into an apartment complex with a swimming pool, and with humour and patience her father taught her to tread water, to swim—first the dog paddle, which made her laugh, and then the crawl. She wanted to learn to dive, but jumping from the diving board seemed like jumping off the second-floor balcony.

"We'll start with something easy," her father had promised. He stood at the side of the pool, bent over at the waist, and extended his arms above his head. "You just let yourself fall in," he said and then he did. When he emerged, wet hair clinging to his forehead, he grabbed the side of the pool and his strong arms raised his body from the water. He'd taught her well. Seven years later, Kate was the star of her swim team. Would he ever see her win another race? Without him, could she even try? "Daddy," she whispered, "you have to come back."

Their first winter in Ottawa, Adam helped their father build a backyard skating rink. Kate wanted to help too, but Adam made it impossible. She hadn't known it then, but trudging up to the crest of the hill she realized it had been all about having their dad to himself. A teenager, hoping soon to get his driver's licence, Adam had needed to prove himself.

And Adam had been at the hospital; he was there when ... Kate couldn't let herself finish the thought, but she couldn't ignore the picture in her mind. She imagined the doctors rushing their father away and her brother as shocked and confused as she was when he broke the news.

How long had he stood in frozen fear—not wanting to leave and yet certain he had to get back to Mom, to be with her when ...?

Ignoring the heat, Kate ran the last block home. Drops of sweat mingled with her tears. Brushing them away, she saw her brother waiting for her on the front lawn. When she reached him, Adam did something she couldn't remember him ever doing before—he hugged her. He hugged her and she felt, not pain, not distress, but relief. "He's alive Katie! He came back to us."

Antony Di Nardo

IT'S NOT TRUE

It's not true that we don't come back
better and stronger and full of vigour
(I meant to write *piss and vinegar*
but obviously something went wrong).
It's not true, I've got proof and so do you.

Look around—the birds are singing
at their appointed places, the fish
are jumping leaps and bounds,
the corner of King and Second
has a newly painted rainbow at its feet
and the gulls, in a poetic sort of way,
have miles to go before they sleep.

Sure, the world may be a wild and transient
place but it's full of hope and hope is fuel
for filling up on *going-further-than-before*.
Why, only yesterday, I was sluggish, bent
and bitter, now I'm full of piss and vinegar.

Alice McMurtry
HEAT OF THE ITALIAN SUMMER (FOR MY GRANDMOTHER)

a girl kisses her medal to Our Lady
prays an end to the war knowing
wishing it away will not make it so

she has not slept since
they crossed from Slovenia to Italy

her farm verdant green to crimson
the burning wood makes a headache
pulse underneath her skull

she must stay awake
if she sleeps, winds up another dead woman
hands of the dead reaching from the roadside
brambles

she passes on her way to church doesn't dare look
ecstasy of saints keeping her from madness

train shudders over tracks
on first watch for
an unanswered question
if journey's end is piled corpses
broken bodies asphyxiated
in the pit

memory violent in its surprise
horse screams, village on fire
focus, God, but she must focus so hard on not dying

her mother with tongue acid taunted Communist partisans
who took her grain the barrels toppled
sparrows rejoiced in manna
"I'd rather the birds have it than you."

her mother's vitriol her inheritance
it rises like a serpent, constricting

James Ronson

SUNBURST

The sunlight slices through the arcing Gehry glass and spills onto the gleaming wooden floor. In all of Toronto, it's one of Shelagh Wright's favourite places—the Galleria Italia, her Olympus. She's curated major exhibitions before, but this will be her final curtain call and it must be her best. She pictures four rooms, one for each classic Greek element.

Room One: Water—the world, indeed life, began with water, and her J. M. W. Turner show will begin and end with his seascapes and riverine landscapes.

Room Two: Earth—represented with Turner's magnificent castles, autumn haystacks, rugged rocks, boulders and avalanches.

Room Three: Fire—a central element will be Turner's eyewitness paintings of the burning of the Houses of Parliament.

Room Four: Air—depicted with Turner's tumbling clouds and sublime threatening skies.

Everything about the show comes together, until the fateful day Shelagh knows will be forever etched in her mind. Catching the early rays of a warm spring day, Shelagh and her husband George are stretched out on their chaise lounges. George sits up, removes his shirt and gazes southward toward the lake.

"What's that?" Shelagh asks.

"To what are you referring?"

"There's something on your back."

"Pigeon shit?"

"I'm serious, George. It's a black blotch of some sort and it doesn't look right." Shelagh rises from her chair and looks closely at his back. "We need to get you to a doctor."

"Now?"

"Yes, George. We're going to the Emergency at Princess Margaret."

"You think it's cancer?"

She nods. Tears filling her eyes.

The cab ride is an anxious dash into the heart of the city. In the hospital, Shelagh paces the floor. Finally, they're directed in to see Dr. Webster.

He examines the lesion and tells them it's called a polypoid. "I'm afraid it's a tell-tale sign of nodular melanoma, but I'm not an oncologist. I'll have you see a Dr. Singh tomorrow morning."

"Melanoma is skin cancer. But nodular? Is that more serious?" asks Shelagh.

Dr. Webster nods. "But as I said, I'm not an oncologist. Dr. Singh will answer your questions. He's one of the best in the field."

Outside the sun is shining. It's the giver of life *and* a killer. Shelagh's mind is racing, filled with thoughts of gloom and doom. For George's sake, she knows she must be strong. She takes his hand. "Let's walk home. Or at least as far as we can get."

George forces a smile. "Yes, let's."

They dine at their favourite restaurant. All is normal, all is not. The sky remains cool and blue as they ascend to the rooftop garden of their condo, a frequent nightly routine. Though nothing is routine now, it seems. Their world has changed. In the privacy of her study, Shelagh calls her boss and arranges to take the week off. Fortunately, George's last course at the university has finished the week before.

It is a restless night for both of them. When George finally succumbs to sleep in the wee hours of the morning, Shelagh slips out of the bedroom to google "nodular melanoma." What she discovers fills her with despair. The more she reads, the worse it gets.

It feels like the ceiling is crashing down upon her and she cries and shakes and shivers through this long dark night of her soul, grateful for just one thing: George isn't here to see this. She must be strong, his Virgil, his guide.

The appointment is only the beginning of their Hell week. Dr. Singh and the pathologist reveal the worst. George is already at Stage Four.

"How long?" asks George. "How long before I exit the stage?"

"That's always the question my patients ask," replies Dr. Singh. "We doctors don't like to answer that."

"You owe me this much," says George. "Now that you've told me nothing can be done."

"All right George, I'll tell you. Less than a year certainly, probably a matter of months."

"Thank you." He glances at Shelagh. "It's best for us both to know."

She marvels at her husband. He's a man of true courage. That evening Shelagh tells George that she plans to resign from her position at the gallery.

"You, my dear, will do nothing of the sort. I won't allow it."

"Everything is in place. The show will continue without me."

"If you'll pardon the pun, let me frame it this way. You've been working like a dog to bring your final show to fruition. I know this news is terrible. But you have your whole life ahead of you. Lil and Joel will need a strong mother to see them through this and I know you possess that strength. I might not be around for the opening, but *you* will. And I will be there in spirit."

When Shelagh begins to cry, he takes her in his arms and begs her to continue the work she started.

"When you put it that way, you leave me no choice."

"Exactly. And if we need to get nursing help, we will. Now there's one more thing that you must promise me."

"George, I don't think I have the will to make any more promises."

"Just one last one."

She sighs. "What is it?"

"I want you to start painting again. I always loved your earlier work from your Toronto days. It was, it *is* beautiful."

"I ... I ... George ... I can't promise you that."

"Then promise me you'll think about it."

"All right."

Spring slides into summer. George is right about everything. His deterioration begins within weeks and they hire help. They set up a hospital bed in the spare room where he can feel the sun streaming down on his face. "It can't kill me now," he says.. "I might as well enjoy it."

Shelagh goes back to work and throws herself into the show. George spends many hours sleeping. Their bedside chats continue after her long days at the gallery. Their children visit as often as they can.

During one of their evening chats George says, "One last promise, Shel."

"What now?" she teases with mock hostility.

"I want you to consider seeing other men after I'm gone."

"Oh, for God's sake, George."

"Not for his sake, for as you know, I don't think he exists. But for your sake."

"Come on, George. I'm pushing seventy. Don' be ridiculous."

"I don't mean for sex. But that would be okay too" he adds with a grin. "I simply mean for companionship."

"I've promised you the moon but I won't promise that."

"All right, a dog then."

Shelagh's incredulous. "You want me to get a dog?"

"You always had dogs growing up and so did I. It will be great company for you."

George dies in his sleep just weeks before the Turner show. Cremation, immediate family and close friends only as he requested. And to fulfill another promise, she scatters his ashes at his favourite park.

The gala opening is a huge affair. It's held in the central assembly room of the gallery. Attendees include the Board members, all the major donors, as well as dignitaries from across the city. Shelagh leads the crowds through "The Classic Elements of J.M.W. Turner." The rooms are awash in splendid yellow light, infused with textured blues and greens, full of magnificent swirling seascapes, wonderful views, and intimate interior paintings. The crowd is buzzing that evening. The next day the press is full of rare praise. The Turner show has turned heads. Attendance exceeds all expectation.

Shelagh plans her retirement for after the close of the show. She's told her colleagues: "No parties, no gifts, no fuss." Of course, many insist on stopping by anyway. With another knock on her office door, Shelagh sighs. "Come in."

"Hi Mom. I've also come to invite you for Christmas," adds Lil. "Joel is coming too."

"Only if I can bring the puppy."

"Puppy? What puppy?"

"I'm picking him up from the breeder next week. He's a Spanish Water Dog. I'm going to call him Sancho." Shelagh doesn't dare tell her daughter that getting a puppy was the more agreeable of George's final wishes.

Christopher Cameron

FALLING FORWARD

I am somewhere between Badwater and Furnace Creek, running. The place names say it all. Heat ripples the air above the road, which ribbons blue-black into the distance. I am hot and tired and my muscles are starting to stiffen up. At this moment there is no place on earth I would rather be.

I was first drawn to California's Death Valley National Park several years ago after I read a book about an event called the Badwater Ultramarathon, a footrace held there every July, when the heat is so oppressive that no one even goes outside during the daytime. I have since come here many times to ride my bike, to run, and to explore, bewitched by the valley's raw beauty and tranquility. For a guy from rural Ontario, used to cool greenness as I run or pedal, this is as exotic as it gets.

I am running across the ancestral lands of the Timbisha Shoshone, a First Nation that has lived in the region for thousands of years. The valley possesses ancient magic that causes the rocks to move on their own in the night, inspires the dunes to sing in the wind, and generates an energy that comes out of the ground and rises through those who walk here. Despite the place's name, a life can come together in this desert, like a song whose words are finally fitted to the tune.

Although the demands of the Badwater Ultra are beyond me, I've wondered for years if it would be physically and mentally possible for me to retrace a small part of the race route on my own. As I flirt with the far end of middle age, the wondering has become more of an urgent need. How many more runs like this are going to be possible?

To be a runner in my sixties is to have more miles behind me than ahead. I own a repertoire of successes and failed attempts: of crouching on the side of a mountain during an ultramarathon in Iceland, trying with red, frozen hands to clear snow from gaiters; of sitting on a path in summertime Florida in a race with many miles left to go, trying to cool swollen feet with ice, wondering how anything can exist in such heat; of dancing effortlessly across the finish line of a marathon or shuffling through the final miles of an Ironman triathlon, resources depleted but not ready to quit. Of enduring.

I've asked a lot of my body, but I've also assumed stewardship of it in a way that I could not imagine when I was a young man. I began running in my thirties, when I thought I had done about everything there was to do; when I had decided that my body was about to begin an inexorable slide down to decrepitude somewhere around age fifty. Something—I'll never know what—told me to give myself one more chance. As much of a struggle as my first 10 K event was, my love affair with endurance running began that day, when I learned that more can be possible today than was possible yesterday.

Over three decades later, I am running all alone through the hottest, driest place on the continent to see what is possible.

My word for the landscape in Death Valley is *thermonuclear*: stark, sunblasted naked, and eerily still. But even here the mountains and the canyons can be palettes of colour and surprise. The sun travelling across the sky during the day creates changing patterns of earthtone in the striated rocks that makes them seem almost edible—dark chocolate, burnt sugar, butterscotch ripple.

Like the scenery, the heat here is breathtaking. The mountains on either side of the valley trap the hot air and funnel the sunlight onto the desert floor. The crackling dryness invades my mouth and lungs like hot gunpowder.

Reactions to people who run long distances usually range from an automatic "You're crazy" to an indifference that would be hurtful if it weren't so thoughtless. I've gotten used to these dismissals and can easily tune out their owners. But no one has ever asked me why I do it.

Because I can? For many years this is how I would have responded to the question. I train hard for an endurance event, and I push myself physically, mentally, and emotionally to get to the finish line. I have earned the right to feel self-satisfied. I do these things because I can.

But really, it's more that I do them because I *can't*. Over the years I've learned to approach each long run with humility and reverence. Because I didn't grow up as a natural runner, I will never be unamazed that I am able to participate in one of these long runs, let alone get to the end of one. And I have discovered that getting to the end is never guaranteed; it is only a possibility.

So I run—to answer the question if anyone ever asks—to see what is possible.

My plan in Death Valley was to cover the 18 miles from Badwater—the lowest point in the Western Hemisphere—to the Furnace Creek Ranch, where my wife and I are staying. But the thermometer at Furnace Creek has been showing temperatures of over 100ºF in the shade every day. *And there is no shade where I am running.* Not a tree, not a telephone pole, not a stick in the sand. Once the sun rises over the cheerfully named Funeral Mountains, she and I are joined until one of us quits. I've decided I'll be content to run as much of my planned distance as I can, with the goal of stopping when I feel I can no longer go on. I have no idea whether the desert will allow me to run all eighteen miles, or whether I'll be stopped after one.

I started running north from Badwater in the relative cool of the desert dawn as the first rays of the sun were touching the mountaintops on the far side of the valley. The road was in the shadow of the mountains to the east, and my plan was to get as many miles as possible under my feet before the sun found me.

Now, hours later, there is not a sliver of shade anywhere. The heat surrounds and infuses me. It rises from the pavement through my legs and body and radiates from my skin. I feel dwarfed by the terrain surrounding me, like a tiny creature crawling across a limitless expanse of sand and rock. Somewhere ahead of me my wife is in the car, waiting at the side of the road. She is meeting me at intervals with electrolytes, water and ice. Her support is all that makes this run survivable.

I'm wearing my hydration vest to provide a supply of water between stops. Before starting my run, I clipped one of my bicycle lights to the vest so that its flashing red pulse might make me more visible to anyone driving down the road. At one point I look down to see that the light is gone; fallen off and lost somewhere along the way.

In contrast to the stunning scenery, the road itself is somewhat boring, with long gentle hills and straight stretches that disappear into the distance like an exercise in perspective. There are mileposts along the way, marking the distance left to Furnace Creek: 16, 15, 14 . . . Once, I rode my bicycle along this road against winds that were so strong I could barely keep upright, counting off those mileposts with excruciating slowness. Today there is not a breath of wind. From time to time I glance across the valley to the 11,000-foot summit of Telescope Peak, sharp against the crystalline air. We hiked to the top just two days ago, and now I think of the snow that we found up there.

As the morning matures, the sun grows more present and I am bathed in everything it can beam down. Although there is no part of me that doesn't feel baked, I'm not covered in sweat; any perspiration I produce dries as soon as it meets the null humidity. I know that there are systems inside my body that are working to keep me from overheating, and I am counting on them now. This is no forest trail; if I don't pay close attention to my hydration and core temperature I can be in life-threatening trouble very quickly.

There is almost no traffic on the road, and most of the time I am utterly alone. If I stop moving and stand still, I can hear wisps of desert song in the distance: wind on bare rock and sand. Sometimes I talk to myself just to make some human sound, and at one point I start singing. Yes, it's The Proclaimers: *500 Miles*.

Running is controlled falling. I shift my body forward by pushing with my back foot, and my front foot hits the road just in time to catch me before I topple onto the pavement. By the time I reach Furnace Creek this process will have been repeated 30,000 times. Surely this is how we all learn to walk—and to live: by reaching forward and trying to catch ourselves before we fall. The simple resilience of that act moves us on.

The hemisphere of my world distills itself into the sand and rocks, the sensation of my feet hitting the melting pavement, the depthless blue sky and the unanswerable sun. On the periphery of my consciousness I am aware of something that I have not felt so intensely or unconditionally for a long time, like a nearly forgotten childhood friend met again after scores of years. Like a dance along a beam of light. Like freedom.

I know the feeling can't last; it is too pure and too absolute. It is as ephemeral as a breath of desert wind and can never be taken away from here. But for this moment, let me run. Let me fall forward for as long as my legs will continue to catch me.

The last mile into Furnace Creek is slightly downhill, and my journey ends on the grassy patch in front of the resort. I take my shoes off and lie down in my first shade in hours, under the palm trees. Amazingly, it's still only mid-morning; the day's real heat has not even begun. The Furnace Creek thermometer reads exactly 100 degrees Fahrenheit. How cool is that?

There is never a question of conquering Death Valley. Those who have lived on this continent for thousands of years have taught us that you don't conquer the land, you don't own it, you don't tame it; you come to an agreement to honour it and to live in harmony with it, or you do not live at all. But if you keep your head in this desert, you are given a chance to hear its song, to experience its power, and to feel its magic. You are granted a possibility.

I feel bad about the bicycle light that I dropped during my run. Written and unwritten laws dictate that you should leave nothing in the pristine environment of the desert. Much later in the day, just before sunset, we drive back down the Badwater Road to look for it. And on the ground right next to Milepost 12, there it is, still flashing away. Like the glint of setting sun on a distant rock, but for now, sufficiently enduring.

Kim Aubrey

THRASHERS

When leaves skitter up the beach
but a gull stays as I walk past
and the tern turns overhead,
slate becomes teal becomes sage
becomes olive.

When the sun sees herself in surf's curl
and surf's shush swallows
the killdeer's frantic alarm,
I stop letting my step be anxious
and the wind brings the lake to my breath.

When one brown thrasher cuts my path
chased by another, scraps with a robin
chest to chest, flicking its cinnamon fan,
I stay and watch the birds go back to their seeking
through old grasses and new growth.

Pam Royl

LISTENING TO THE LAND

Standing upon our piece of land high atop a hill, I feel a familiar deepening within me, a connection felt only in this place. My mind drifts across time, imagining what this land has endured. There is something about this acreage, with its border of dense forest, that makes one feel the vibration of its history. I wonder what it has witnessed, and what it has survived at the hands of those who claimed it as their own. What was it like *before* they came?

I try to sense what this land would tell me if it could. Would it speak of the plundering of its trees for lumber and the clear-cutting to make way for crops and grazing livestock? Today you might look at the great expanse of the hills and gasp, "But look at all those trees." And I would tell you that before the European settlers, it was a dense forest of ancient pine trees, much like the old growth forests that still exist in Northern Ontario and British Columbia.

After the settlers stripped the trees away, erosion caused such destructive flooding that the Ganaraska Region Conservation Authority was created and took charge of reforestation, planting much of the lush forest of the Northumberland Hills. With this help, the land renewed itself, coming back from the brink of devastation.

In the city I lived in years ago, I never thought about what used to be on the land. It seemed impossible that anything existed before the giant buildings and the smothering of the land beneath asphalt and concrete, chasing the remnants of forests into ravines and parks. Perhaps the disharmony and immediacy of the city made it impossible to ever ponder echoes of the past.

Now I stand on our land nestled high up in the hills, inhale the clear sweet air, and take in the majestic view to the east and south. Each year, holes appear within our forest view as new houses sprout, slowly dissolving the green, giving the impression it has been set upon by some mysterious rot.

The wooded land behind our property has never been developed. We heard it's unattractive for development, with no easy access road; but we expect any day a builder will start tearing down the trees to make way for more houses.

There is a stone wall that runs along the back of our land, buried under mounds of leaves and deadfall. Perhaps early settlers built it as a border fence for farmland or a roadway. Decades ago, our land was the site of a quarry. I envision the land stripped of its trees once more—this time to take its bedrock. After the quarry was gone, the Township sold the property as building lots. The land was restored from a dissipated gravel pit into our current neighbourhood, thick with trees and shrubs. A shallow pond sits at its centre—presumably where the bottom of the pit once existed—and is fed by a creek running underground from Rice Lake. This pond is a vibrant natural habitat, home to an ever-expanding flock of geese and blue heron, armies of frogs and toads, and nests of turtles.

Behind our house, at the south end of the forest, there is a steep decline to scrubland, and a further descent to a creek. Perhaps this cliff was the result of rock being gouged out of the quarry. Now the area is a transitway for small herds of white-tailed deer, fox and coyotes, and the home to squirrels, chipmunks, rabbits, raccoons and skunks.

I listen to the chorus of honking geese, cawing crows, trilling robins, chattering squirrels and buzzing insects. Above it all is the faint thrum of the highway and the occasional whistle of a train.

The sense of *Before* is so strong when gazing at the forest. The land has withstood mankind twice, that I know of, and is reborn each spring, rising once again from the frozen depths of winter, filling us with the joy of a new beginning. And I thank this land for giving so much after all that has been taken.

Esther Sokolov Fine

IN THE COVID MARKETPLACE

Radishes and turnips speak bitterness to parsnips and carrots;
today it is winter and hope is masked. We eat snow for lunch,
and sing for our supper at separate tables.

God has no title or pronoun, *she* is wrong, *he* is wrong,
one and *they* are also wrong. Can there still be song,
or must all become still?

If God has no shape, no weight, no size nor sides, then
round is wrong, square is wrong, tri and bi are also wrong.
Can there still be sunsets, moonrises, calories and scales?

If God has no past or future, no mortgages or rents,
must we live and die in present tents, or can there be
a safer sense of more and less?

What if God became bored, tired, sick of stuff, or
stuck in bed with wreckage on the floor,
a model of procrastination?

What if God forgot, or energized, began another project,
chose to take a swim - drown all sorrows, heedless of
unfinished beings lying on a frayed carpet?

Perhaps God took offense at words and deeds,
or a broken arm stopped creation midstream
and couldn't be redeemed.

God may be lying in hospital awaiting oxygen,
dreaming of a nurse with ice chips. In congested corridors,
who hears God's prayers?

Or maybe God has gambled and already lost,
soil traded for plastic, oil wells spilling, silver tarnished,
fools' gold - just dust unaccounted for?

There is a bill to be paid, to be ignored,
to be argued, to be passed. When eviction comes,
where will a homeless God find food?

Perhaps an editor awaits, with elegance, energy
and a robust vision of what life might become.
If re-vision could drive survival, what then?

Shane Joseph

RESILIENCE

We were gathered in a semi-circle, which was reassuring; a single line would suggest moving towards an inevitable precipice, and a falling off, one by one. We were also mercifully allowed to remove our masks upon seating.

The facilitator was a jovial fellow in his mid-seventies; a pro, I gathered, stepping up to help this bunch of sods navigate the next twenty years of their lives until death or disability rendered them irrelevant. Irrelevant—that was in the cards as soon as I sold the travel agency and decided to do what all seniors do: enjoy retirement with lots of golf, cheap travel and mornings at Tim Hortons for donuts and coffee.

I was now part of a group reduced to talking about global issues we could do nothing about, or putzing around in social media on home computers, absorbing a million conspiracy theories about how the government and Big Pharma were screwing us. But there was no travel these days due to the pandemic, the golf courses were closed, and Tim's had only drive-thru, for which I did not have a car.

I looked around at my fellow retirees. About a dozen or so nondescripts, and a few who caught my attention: the vivid redhead with an overly-generous bust and painted lips, wearing high heels that didn't look like they could support her girth; the guy in a trilby who had a tan that seemed to come from a lamp; the chap with the portable oxygen tank and tube running into his nose who used his walker to sit down, placing the tank in the walker's carry basket—he looked the youngest of us all. The others only came to life when they spoke, if they spoke.

"I'm Jim," our jolly facilitator began, as soon as we had settled down with flat coffee (certainly not from Tim's) and cookies that tasted as if they had been baked for diabetics. "Welcome to the 'Retiring Well' series organized by our generous Community Centre. I've been retired for over twenty years and have been running these sessions for ten. I must tell you that these are the best years of your life. In fact, I start these sessions by getting everyone to say 'This is the best day of my life.'"

"Bullshit," said the redhead. "Never saying that."

"Heh, heh," went the trilby.

Oxygen Guy gasped, "I can hardly breathe. How ... how are these ... the best years?"

"Well, we'll get into it. Let's introduce ourselves first," said Jim.

We went around offering names. The redhead was Jayne, reminding me of the buxom Jayne Mansfield, except that this Jayne did not have the signature platinum blonde of the starlet, and she was at least fifty-five. Trilby was George, and Oxygen Guy was Tom.

"Now, let's share our life stories. Fred, why don't we begin with you?" Jim was looking at me.

I cleared my throat. "Not much to tell, really. Divorced, former business owner. Sold the shop due to the pandemic. Children flown the nest. Looking for how to navigate a world where everything is fake, Photoshopped and attention-deprived."

"Trust issues?" Jim asked.

I grunted. "Huh. How do you decide which politician or newspaper is telling the truth anymore, or what brand of vaccine to take? We are drifting into retirement in a fog of make-believe."

"Do you have a pension?" Jayne interrupted, eyeing me.

"Only whatever I put into my RRSP during a good year. That, and what the government gives out—just enough to put food on the table for myself."

"Then I wouldn't marry you," she said, winking, yet the toss of dismissal was evident. "I'm looking for a Sugar Daddy. It's my only route to survival."

"What did you do, Jayne?" Jim asked, his eyes showing keen interest. I even detected dregs of lust on his face.

"Actress. Theatre. Commercials. I once played in a Hollywood movie."

"Which one?"

"I'm not saying."

"Who was your male lead?" Jim was pressing, his eyes widening.

"It was a walk-on part. My agent was a slime-bucket. Only wanted to get me in bed with producers so I could get the bigger parts, and he could get a bigger slice of my earnings. I left Hollywood and returned to Canada."

"I remember you in the beer commercial," George interrupted, his voice a lazy drawl.

Jayne fluttered her lashes at him. "You do?"

"Yeah. You looked great. I drank a lot of beer afterwards."

"Maybe we should go out for a pint after we finish here?"

"You'll have to come to my place, honey. Pubs are closed."

"Sure."

"Ahem ..." A neglected Jim cleared his throat. "Let's get on with our life stories, shall we? George, since you've been so ... so forthcoming, tell us about yourself."

"Sure. Printing was my gig."

Jayne chuckled. "Did you have to wear that trilby on sales calls?"

George doffed the hat, revealing a lush growth of grey, curly hair. "It helped impress customers. Gave me the Leonard Cohen look. But then Cohen died and the trilby went out of fashion. So did printing. Everything went online."

Tom was waving his hand as if he had an emergency, and when Jim allowed him to speak next, he looked grateful. "Thanks ... I run out of air suddenly … so … I would like to get my piece done while my lungs hold up."

"Go ahead, Tom," Jim said.

"I … have … long COVID."

"Sorry to hear that."

"I worked in the big warehouse down the road where everything is automated." Tom stopped to catch his breath. Then he continued. "All we had to do was run faster and faster, to keep up with increasing orders after COVID broke. And we were breathing in each other's air. A lot of us came down with the virus."

I was curious. "Pardon me for asking, Tom, but you look pretty young. Forties? Why are you in this group for retired people?"

"I *retired*. No more running after parcels for me, I told myself. Parcels are for deadbeats. And there's more than enough of them. COVID clogged my lungs, but opened my brains."

"How will you live?" Jayne asked.

"I'm living with Mom. She's got Dad's survivor pension. When she dies, the house is mine. I'll rent out the basement and live on the income."

"I wish I had a Sugar Mommy," Jayne cooed.

"I thought you wanted a Sugar *Daddy?*" George said.

"I'll take either. My profession is dead too, these days. No plays, no movies, no roles for people like me whose boobs are beginning to sag. And no pensions."

"You don't sag to me," George said leaning forward in his chair staring at her cleavage. Jayne fluttered her eyes at him.

"Ahem …" Jim cleared his throat even louder this time, and I thought he was going to administer punishment by consigning these two to the dunces' corner, or better, send them away to drink that "beer" together. "We must really move onto the others …"

Other stories poured out. They had been teachers ("not going back to those COVID petri-dishes when schools re-open"); librarians ("libraries are closed, what's the use?—took early retirement"); clerical workers ("everything went online—accounting, projects, HR, meetings—can't stand that 'Zoom' thing"); gig workers ("the gigs dried up"); and consultants ("my skills became obsolete in a virtual economy"); even a nurse ("... burned out. Fucking COVID!"). I realized that many had retired post-pandemic. I looked at our bouncy Jim and decided to rattle him.

"Hey Jim, you seem to have weathered retirement well. How did you manage it?"

Jim puffed his chest. "Well, I retired at fifty-five, when the number of years of service plus your age added to eighty. Indexed pension. Government job."

Jayne pounced on him immediately. "Yay, the Sugar Daddy I've been looking for!"

Jim pulled back with his hands raised in protest. "Whoa! I'm married."

"Haven't you heard of a mistress? Hollywood was full of them."

"Can barely afford the wife, Jayne. Budgeting—that's what we all have to do. I'll be teaching budgeting in a future class."

"Great," Tom said. "Budgeting only applies if you have money that stretches beyond one visit to the grocery store."

"Or pays the rent," the ex-gig worker piped up.

Tom seemed to have got a fresh boost of oxygen, for he spoke uninterrupted now. "I worked for the government for a while. But there were only contract jobs by the time I came along. Jim, guys from your generation are like those tenure-track university professors."

"Don't tell me about those bastards," one of the quieter ones, who had identified as another gig worker, exploded. "Those kiss-asses get paid a living wage to do dick-all, while we part-timers are hired to do their grunt jobs in the lecture halls. All they do is sit inside cloistered offices, screw their students, and dream about the future of things. In all their wisdom, did they forecast this pandemic? My ass!"

"Now, now. We must mind our language and be respectful of the Other," Jim said raising his hands as if to quell this revolt of the peasants. There was a crease on his brow. "I do appreciate that times are a bit ... different ... now. And difficult. Each cycle of employment and retirement brings its unique set of challenges."

"But you ain't qualified to teach us about our challenges. You had it darned easy in your time." It was the retired nurse speaking. "Do you know what it's like to work a twelve-hour shift intubating patients who are going to die anyway, dressed in a hazmat suit that's reeking of your sweat and other people's pus, phlegm, and vomit, while wearing a mask that's beyond disgusting. And then being told you have to work another shift because your replacement tested positive and had to go into quarantine?"

Jim had lost his ebullience by this time and looked like he was checking the exits from which to beat a retreat.

I intervened. "Let's give Jim a break. It's not his fault we had a pandemic, or that the system is screwing us. He's only trying to help."

Jim sighed and sat down for the first time since we had arrived. He looked down at his shoes. The circle quieted down, as if having pity for him, the most privileged one of all of us.

Finally, Jim spoke. "You know, you are right. I am *not* qualified. It's getting harder to run these sessions. I try to spread hope, but the waves of despair sweeping in from people like you 'quite o'er-crows my spirit,' as they say. I think we should call it a day. Perhaps, we can reconvene next week at this time for Session Two and see how you feel. I hope you come back, because I have much to teach you."

I took pity on him. "Jim, at least, give us your magic recipe for retirement before we break. That might help us decide whether we want to return."

"Well, thank you, Fred." Jim stood up, holding his hand up, asking for quiet. Then he cleared his throat. "Since you asked ... er ... since Fred here asked ... let me tell you my recipe: *you've gotta be happy and grateful, no matter what.* From here on, life will be uncertain. Every day will make us weaker and more things will start to give way." He looked at Jayne's generous bosom as he said it, and she pushed her boobs up in reflex action.

"Mine is not a *magic* recipe, but a survival strategy. Resilience. All I can tell you is that you are going to die. So why not make this next chapter pleasant? Yes, I have financial security. More than all of you, it appears, from what you have shared today. But what the hell does that mean if I don't have my health? I've been dealing with prostate cancer for five years. Yeah, I don't show it. Why do I need to show it and make everyone around me miserable? That's my challenge."

The room was quiet now. Looks of anger had softened into guilt, pity and embarrassment. Then Tom rasped. "You can join my club, Jim. I got my Momma's money, but I got no health either."

Nervous laughter broke the tension.

Jim continued. "I'm not finished. I told Jayne here that I was married. That's correct. I *was*. Wife, who was diabetic, died of COVID last month. I got off with a bad chest cold that mercifully left. Sorry about your Long COVID, Tom—I seemed to have been spared that, at least."

"I'm really sorry for your loss, Jim," the nurse said. "I know what it's like for families cut off from loved ones who are breathing their last in the ICU. I had to break the news more than a few times to family members."

"Thank you, but I haven't finished. My only son, who was in the military, got killed in Afghanistan during the pandemic, leaving his wife and two children bereft. That pension I spoke about—half of it goes to help my dead son's family now."

I went up to Jim and placed my hand on his shoulder. "Jim, it looks like you need us more than we need you. Why do you run these sessions with such false bravado when you are going through so much yourself?"

He bit back the tears. "Because I *have* to. It's my only affirmation that this is still a good world. Don't you see? If you give in, you give up, and you're done."

"Is today still the best day of your life?"

"It has to be. Because I don't know what disaster is coming tomorrow. Every day *has* to be the best one. Don't you get it?"

Jayne picked up her bag and stood up. "This is getting too heavy. I'm out of here. Sorry Jim, for calling you a Sugar Daddy and all. Me and my big mouth. I think we need a beer. Several beers."

"Sounds like a good idea," George said, rising too and straightening his trilby. He winked at Jayne.

Chairs scraped tentatively, and people stood up to leave. Masks reappeared over faces. Jim sat down in his chair and waved at us. "Goodnight, everyone. I'll see whoever comes back next week. We'll cover 'Financial Planning on a Fixed Income' as our first real exercise, now that we've broken the ice with each other. And thanks for sharing, and listening."

***

I stayed behind after the others left. There were some things on my mind that needed clarifying: a look here, a sigh there, a recovery too soon. Jim busied himself straightening his papers and putting them back in his briefcase.

"Government job, indexed pension, you said, eh? Did you work for CSIS?" I asked.

"No," he laughed quietly. "But all governments are labyrinthine."

"None of that shit really happened to you, did it?"

He didn't look up. "No."

"Then why did you lie to us?"

"I learned early in my career that the only way to put out a fire was to start a bigger one."

"Like those politicians, eh? You think anyone will trust you once word gets out that you lied to the group?"

"The bit about the government job and the pension was true."

"But the other pieces ... your personal tragedies. You were wrenching our hearts out."

"Doesn't everyone lie these days? You said it earlier. Politicians, medical experts, the media. Bosses, husbands and wives—everyone lies. And yet we cling to the hope that they must be honest, if only to keep our sanity and continue living."

"But I thought you were of the last of the honest ones. The first half of the post-war boomer generation that upheld a just society in this country. No?"

"Yes. But everything is fluid now. I had to learn how to navigate this post-truth world we consequently helped create, or get run over. My cohort inadvertently invented 'Tefloning,' where lies are standard practice. Everyone's an actor now. So, we only have good actors and bad actors today, not honest ones who build just societies."

"Is that also one of the classes in this series?"

"The final lesson, during which, confessions for lies told will be made and reparations sought. This whole country is about that, isn't it? Hope you'll stick around."

"You've got my attention. I *will* return, especially for that last lesson. 'Tefloning' is something I have to learn."

Jim winked. The ebullience was back, the tears had vanished—they had been as fake as Jayne's breasts or George's tan.

"It would be nice to have one student, at least, who gets the message and completes the course," he said, clicking his briefcase shut.

"The others will find their way back here too, I bet, even if only to hear more sob stories from you. Sympathy attracts, like moths to the candle flame."

"Or sheep to the slaughter. I didn't think I would have to use it so early in the course though. But this was a tough bunch. How did you catch on to me?"

"You were too slick."

"Practice makes perfect, they say. I guess, I was *too perfect*, eh?"

"You need a new 'story.'"

"And yet they say, 'A lie oft repeated becomes a truth.'"

I slipped on my mask. "Well, I'm must be off to navigate this fake world."

"Remember, if you give in, you give up, and you're done. If lies help to fight other lies, or if you can lie to tell a higher truth—do it."

"That *was* your magic recipe, wasn't it?"

He merely smiled. "See you next week, Fred."

Katie Hoogendam

THE HOLE

My son, nine years old
last summer dug a hole.
Sheer winsomeness, no purpose
he maneuvered the shovel
with the grace of a Zen master.
No agenda.
Nearly eight feet deep
the hole makes a perfect grave.
For some time, we awaited the body
but there are too many bodies now
and our grief, once buried,
simply resurrects.
Spring will be here soon
and I watch the mailbox daily
for the arrival of our seeds
ready my body to bend
dig.
Even now, I can see
one hole
will not suffice
for all
that needs planting.

mia burrus

ROLLING ALONG

Invoking resilience as bounce
puts the onus on the rubber lady
to recover, fails
to acknowledge the roles
that lovers or other strangers,
muses or dancing partners,
play in bouncing back.

Perhaps less bounce and more
the glancing click of billiard balls
is a way to get through
on your own.
Clack! and carom away
in baize silence, drop
into a pocket, perhaps.
(Silently await the five fingers
of love to reach in and say,
No! return to play.)

India Rubber or Bakelite,
is it the economy,
the integrity of the sphere
which imparts resilience?
Nothing to pinch, grab,
snag, no sharp corners
to turn into weapons,
only smooth silence
and the wile to resile.

Lynn C. Bilton

GREENER ACRES

"You bought a farm?!" I heard this remark frequently in the days following my decision. It's not a common choice for a thirty-year-old single female.

When I stopped at the roadside on my first drive-by of the property, however, I remember exclaiming out loud, "This is it!" The old red-brick farmhouse and large red barn reminded me of the dairy farm where my brothers and I were raised. I had found my new home.

For seven years, my husband and I had run a florist shop and greenhouse operation in Southern Ontario. We rebuilt each of the original greenhouses and updated the entire undertaking, which had been established many years prior by his parents.

With 10,000 square feet under glass, a market garden and a busy roadside stand, in addition to the florist shop and wire service, there was always planning to be done. Part-time staff included several adults plus a flock of students. It was a daily beehive of activity. The surroundings of warmth, colour, plants and cut flowers in a tropical setting offered a welcoming work environment.

That perfect picture came to a halt when my husband died unexpectedly in June 1987, three months shy of our tenth wedding anniversary. My life as I had known it came to a jarring halt.

I was already teetering on the edge. Not only had my husband died, but his parents and my eldest brother's wife had also passed away in recent years. It was a time of prolonged grieving.

I closed the flower shop and went to stay with friends who lived in a tranquil country setting. Being offered this refuge by the kindest of folks helped to mend my broken spirit. Sometime during my stay at this rural retreat, I realized I needed to start fresh.

The farm would be my new beginning.

My parents and family helped me move into my new home on a cold February day. My dad and I walked the property and started our plans to get my new operation up and running.

My purchase was long before the days of home inspections. On the second morning I woke and discovered the waterlines in the house were frozen. I called the previous owners and asked for advice. They arranged for another neighbour to stop by with a portable welder. My water source was a cistern under the barn. My neighbour attached a clamp to the waterline in the barn and another clamp to the waterline in the house and they "zapped" the line to unfreeze it. The previous owner had omitted telling me I should keep a tap dripping to avoid freeze-ups. Sometime later, I discovered that the zapping process was illegal and could have started a fire. Digging a proper well moved to the top of my list. My new learning curve had begun.

Less than one month after I took possession, my father died. My planning partner was gone. It was a devastating blow, but I corralled my inner strength, determined to move forward and honour the plans my dad and I had discussed.

One issue that needed to be addressed promptly was the ancient electrical setup. If I plugged in the kettle and toaster at the same time, the main breaker would flip. This required a walk to the hydro pole partway down the laneway where the switch was located. The arrangement was *not* convenient.

I quickly found a full-time job. Good thing too, as I had hired a gentleman to begin my much-needed renovations. He called me at work one day and asked, "Are you sitting down?" I knew the news couldn't be good. The septic tank was the original, installed decades earlier. It was made of bricks with a wooden top. The wood had rotted and caved in, which caused the contents to back up into my basement. By the time I arrived home from work, the contractor had called a plumber with a backhoe who was in the process of digging out the original system and preparing for a new septic tank. Neither of us were happy campers that day.

A few months later, I arrived home from work to discover eleven jack-posts supporting the dining room ceiling. When the back portion of the house was added, the builder had cut through the wall but had never incorporated a support beam. In other words, the second story had no means of reinforcement. Friends began asking me if I had ever watched the movie *The Money Pit*.

Fencing was another priority as my plan was to raise beef cattle. With the help of one brother, I purchased a large quantity of century-old split rails to achieve that "rustic" look. Another brother knew a gentleman with a transport trailer to deliver them. I hired a team of students to build the fence via a "piecework" agreement that required my watchful eyes. One day I arrived home from work and spotted a spindly post planted at a fence corner. I stopped my truck to chat with the lads. "No, that won't work," I told them. "You see, a corner post acts as an anchor post. You should choose one of the biggest posts."

I wanted to raise not only beef cattle, but all my own food and be somewhat self-sufficient. I purchased chickens to raise for meat in addition to laying hens and pigs. And I maintained a large vegetable garden. At times I boarded a few of my neighbour's overflow of Clydesdales.

Since I didn't own any implements, I hired neighbours to complete any tractor work. This included cutting and baling hay. Once the day was set to bale hay, phone calls went out to my city friends to help bring in the harvest. The project became an annual party because I offered a BBQ supper to celebrate the end of our workday.

Obstacle after hurdle sprang up in my path, yet I lived and blossomed on my farm for seventeen years. Nothing deterred my dream. I thrived on the trials and learned from them. My losses during this time were more than just detours—they were the building blocks to a stronger me. My tears of grieving gave way to joy from my sense of accomplishment.

I learned that life rarely follows the path you envision; there will always be diversions. It's how you tackle the snags that makes the difference. The encouragement from my family and friends gave me strength, and I am forever grateful. They were beside me during my grieving *and* my healing process.

My farm was a lot of work in a physical sense but it served as the therapy I required to heal. One day I knew I was ready to move on to a new opportunity.

On the day I left my farm for the last time, I walked down the laneway to gather the mail from my mailbox. The timing coincided with my mail lady's daily delivery. She had heard I was moving and wished me well, smiling as she drove off. I smiled too. I left with a feeling of fulfillment and peace, proud of my achievements and ready to accept my next challenge in life.

Ted Amsden

ENDURING LOCKDOWN

it was plain insane
trying to make anything great again

so many tears during texting

the money strain
that mood swung
made of investments undue pain

though I TikTok'd
like my mother watched
Wheel of our MisFortune

everyday the germaphobia opera
washing cereal boxes macabre

no wiser because of sanitizer
just tasked to mask

do not touch
stand in line
keep your distance
hold your breath

made the most of
my thirty seconds
with the checkout clerk

then repaired to despair
home alone

the thorns of roses
bled tears that year

John Unruh

SHAE AND THE IMP

They say you don't know unless you try. Right? But oh my God. Trying. What if that's the thing. What if you can't even try. What if you're just not able. Or too scared. If every time you give it a go, some crazy, maddened bugger stands in front of you, knocks you back on your ass and pins you like a bug on a cork or hobbles you like a dumb calf and makes you squeal for your mother.

What then?

Not physically, mind you. I'm not talking about some actual fey prick jumping out of a shadow to stand in all the dimensions of reality, balling up his fists to beat me down. I'm talking about something that feels real. So real you'd swear it was something physical. But it's inside instead. And it's me.

When I was growing up, my half-brother Faisal called it Shaitaan, the devil jinn. That's from his dad. I call it the imp. That's from mine.

Faisal could always see it happening, too, even though he was smaller than me. Younger, I mean. He was smart that way. He could see the imp, sitting on my shoulder, whispering into my ear. He knew by the way I'd go all still and how my eyes went all far away and backwards at the same time, like the imp had pressed a pause button in my brain to stop the motion of me and turn my eyes around—so I had to pay attention while he grew whatever fear happened to be inside of me and used it to punch me in the gut over and over until my breathing went ragged.

I would tell my mother when it got like this. At least at first. And bless her heart, she'd listen every time and then run her fingers through my hair to sweep it back out of my eyes and she'd smile and say something like we all feel it, Shae. It's just nerves. Now stop your worrying. Go out and play with your brother ya' gammy turd. And Faisal and I would go out and play and most times I'd feel better for it. But sometimes I didn't.

It went like this all through public school.

Jesus, I wish it were just nerves.

By high school, I'd pretty much given up trying. I mean, what was the point? I did my work. I kept my grades up. But I'd given up trying to become something. Or care about anything. Instead, I watched. I saw everyone carefully building their dreams and such and I marvelled all the while that they could do it. How did they find the strength to dream when dreams were nothing but food for the imp? Why would you feed a creature like that if you didn't have to? And I didn't understand why they didn't see it like that, because at the time I believed everyone had an imp, and that they were all exactly like mine. That no one was any different from me. And I thought, how could they be so ignorant? How could they dare to hope for anything good when the imp was always there, watching and waiting and ready to pounce at a moment's notice?

Then, in college, I met Georgie. My glowing, bright light. When I was with her, like truly—in the moment and present with her—the imp could not be found. And this was a form of magic to me. So, you'll understand why I fell in love with her, and how easily she became my anchor. The place I could go to feel safe and nurtured and free when home and Mom and Faisal were so far away.

And it was a thing of beauty when we met too. A moment any cinephile would swoon over. The first moment I looked into her sweet, sweet eyes I knew she wanted me as much as I wanted her, and I knew I would do anything to keep her. Whatever it took. Which was a wonderful feeling to have but also the most frightening thing in the world. When she was there, I shone for her, like I've never shone before. But when she wasn't, the imp would come again, because it knew I had something to lose and there was nothing it liked better than helping me lose something.

So, trying. There's still a lot you can do, even when you've given up trying. And I mean the day-to-day when I say this. But that's just a given, isn't it? That's where the living is. Waking up. Feeding Georgie. Eggs and juice. Coffee. Making love on the front porch with the curtains drawn just enough to keep the neighbours at bay. Dinner. Laundry. Laughing. Exploring Georgie every night. I mean, my God, she was a never-ending story and still is, even after all these years. Each touch familiar. No touch ever the same.

But the day to day can't sustain us, can it. At some point you have to do more. You have to pay your fair share if you want to keep a front porch with curtains and a home and a person you love or, maybe even one day, people you love.

Not that Georgie ever made me feel any of this was true. But that's how love is, isn't it? You always want to do more. And more is better. Right? That's what they say.

So, I tried again, despite the imp. I dreamed. For Georgie. I bartered an unfinished degree against a new one that would lead to a career. And I felt good like I always do at the start of something. I thought, this is it, Shae, you're about to arrive. You're going to make something of yourself and make Georgie proud.

But the imp had different plans, of course. And like everything I ever tried before, it went sour as the realities piled into my arms, brick after brick, until I couldn't hang on to them anymore and they all came crashing down around my feet, chipping at the edges of my nails and bruising the tender skin on the tops of my toes and cracking the bones beneath.

I was nearly finished when I quit, too. The degree, that is. That's the sad part. But there I was. Broken and shattered, angry and ruined, with Georgie cuddled into my side to console me so I could turn into her and weep and weep, what's wrong with me, why can't I do it. Why can I never do it.

She told me we'd be fine, of course. She had a good job. We'll always have what we need, she said. I was enough for her just the way I was.

Every day. More than enough. She told me I was the reason she laughed and sang and saw joy and wonder in everything and everyone, because that was my power, all the rest of it be damned. And she told me, even then, that I didn't have to try so hard to be more than I was. I just didn't.

So, I made myself believe it was true. But at the same time I could feel that secret part of me working, too, trying not to think about the moment she would leave my side, even to go pee or brush her teeth, so she wouldn't have to come back and catch me talking through the backs of my eyes again like a moth at a candle, greedy for the imp's burn.

And it might have been a mistake to hide it from her, what was happening inside of me, but I just didn't want her to see it. Even though she saw it anyway. Even though she knew the imp was there, because it's not easy to hide something like that when someone loves you and knows you better than you know yourself.

Or maybe it wasn't a mistake at all, because when I look back on it, I'm pretty sure that was the moment that ended up bringing Jasper into our lives. Or at least the start of it. That was the moment Georgie just said it, out of the blue. You have so much love in you, Shae. Just share it. It's all you need to do.

He came to us at the perfect time, Jasper did. Georgie and I were ready as we'd ever be. At the age where the need to nurture something falls on you like a warm bath, all unexpected and pleasant, though maybe not nearly from the direction you might have guessed.

By this time, Georgie had helped me tuck away the hollowness that followed my second aborted degree. I'd taken a part-time job at the grocery and I was content enough with the work but wouldn't miss it if it had to go, which it did in the end.

The adoption agency approached us after we'd successfully fostered a couple of cheeky whelps in an emergency situation and proved we could do it. They told us we had the knack of it when maybe others didn't so much. So, we said yes and just like that we were parents.

Jasper. He was good for both of us. A singularity of need that ate up care and spewed out love so Georgie and I were soaked in it. Enamoured. Besotted. You name it. His challenges became our anthems. His victories our glories. He was the centre of our being and the extent of it, to the point that nothing else really mattered.

And for a few short years it wasn't even about trying at all. It was just about doing. Which I could only liken to a form of heaven. Something impossible and satisfying. A way of stepping out of time with all your happiness so you could enjoy it in peace for what it was.

But the thing is you can't step out of time. Even if it feels like you can. And the day finally came when we sent Jasper off to school and I went home with tears drying in my eyes and conversations with the working moms lapping at my ears.

So, Shae, they said, what are you going to do now that you've some time on your hands? And that's how it started again. There with the working moms and a little pinprick of conversation that let the darkness inside of me seep through once more.

The first weeks after school started weren't so bad. Georgie and I adjusted to Jasper's new routine and I managed to fill my days well enough. But then Faisal stepped in and asked if I would join him in a little side venture because I had some time on my hands and he could really use the help.

And as soon as he did—as soon as he said the words—I could feel it coming again, just like that. The pinprick turned into a kind of burrowing, like someone picking at an eggshell from the inside. And of course I ignored it because the shell felt strong. And I felt strong. And I thought I could do it. I really did.

When Faisal arrived to pick me up that first day I could see Georgie, in my mind, standing behind me, hoping and praying. But I couldn't help myself. I just couldn't. Daft as the pickle that fell from the bowl. And off we went, Faisal all smiles and assurances and secret nods to Georgie and winks that said it would all be fine, just give her a chance.

So, she did.

It took some spit and shine from old St. Cajetan, but the first year with Faisal went really well. He had a knack for the business end. I had a knack for the work, the day to day, and could lose myself in it for hours with little thought or worry. We were a good team this way. After work at the end of the day, I had Jasper to care for with Georgie at night. And this all kept the imp at bay, even though I could feel it still, picking and feeling around, looking for a thread to hang on to so it could pull itself out of its shell and start weaving again.

Then the day came when Faisal landed his dream job and told me he was leaving our little partnership—that it was all up to me now, and not to worry because I would be fine. And I looked at him and smiled and nodded my head in agreement so he'd believe that I believed it. But that was it. The panic set in and the imp found its thread. It got its hooks in right and proper. I fought as hard as I could but it was no use.

Later that night, after tucking Jasper in, I lay down in bed with Georgie. I felt the warmth of her pressed all up behind me, her arm draped over my shoulder, elbow nestled between my breasts, hand playing with the short hairs over my ear at the side of my head. But I might as well have been on the other side of the planet I was so deep into the backs of my eyes.

And Georgie knew it, of course. That I wasn't going to make it. She could feel it happening without even having to look. And I knew she felt it. And for the first time in my life, I felt the sheer weight of me. How it fell on her.

You need to find a way to see that you're enough, she said. And I'll bless her always for finding the strength to do it.

I nodded my head, there on the pillow. I felt her forehead move against the back of my scalp when I did it, and I knew what I had to do.

I need help, I said.

And Georgie nodded, too, forehead to scalp. And that was that.

So, you wouldn't believe what a little work can do. A little trying in the right place and the right time.

I know. Don't laugh.

I'm still amazed when I think back to it. How sharp the turn was when it came. How much I might have lost if I hadn't the sense or luck or whatever it was to see the cliff approaching.

And I don't want to say I'd been a fool for not getting help sooner, but I was. At the same time, I know there's just no way of getting around it. Sometimes you need to live through a thing to get to a place where you realize you don't want it in your life anymore. A place where you can find the strength in yourself and through the people you love to finally do what it takes to deal with it, or even just find a way to manage it. It's the simplest truth.

So, trying. Not trying. I'm not sure anymore if that's even a thing. If you're breathing, you're trying. That's about all there is to it. And maybe, in the end, all we need to do is give ourselves a little credit for it.

Melissa Thorne

POETRY PERSEVERING DESPITE MOTHERHOOD

Ink on paper
      "Mommy! Look at this…"
representing stolen
      The baby's crying…
moments of
      The dog peed on the floor…
solitude.
      The toddler hit the baby…
Furtive scribbles
      Now, they're both crying…
that become
      Let's put the baby down for a nap.
incoherent
      The dog's chewing on the curtains…
the longer
      "Mommy! I'm hungry…"
they're left alone.
      "No! I don't want grapes!"
They made sense
      "Mommy! I dropped my Cheerios…"
once.
      The baby's awake…
Perhaps some coffee
      Where'd I leave my coffee?
will revive

"Mommy! Where's my car?"

my synapses,

"MOMMY! I WANT MY CAR!"

and provide

"NO! NOT THAT CAR!"

clarity.

Sloppy, gooey, baby kisses…

Eventually, words coalesce

High pitched giggles…

into an entity entirely

"I love you Mommy!"

my own.

Ken Morden

THE ADVERTISEMENT

Mike Biggar, wearing his number 32 Toronto Maple Leafs jersey, found the site on his laptop. The Leafs had fifteen minutes to get a goal and tie the Canadiens, but Mike couldn't wait. He'd sent Isaac to bed right after receiving the phone call, and now he was staring at a home page that claimed the site was one of the most popular on the internet.

Mike scrolled until he found the familiar face, and clicked on it. "Holy shit," he muttered to himself. A naked teenaged girl appeared, full screen. Was it really her? Damn it, it couldn't be. Mike closed his laptop, then closed his eyes. What should he do? What could he do?

His dilemma had begun with a cell call at the start of the third period. "Hi Freddy, what's up?" he asked his warehouse assistant.

"Hey Mike, you're probably watching the game, but I, um, found something you should know about. Something personal. I'm sending you a link to a website. It's not good, but it's something you need to see."

The link came into his phone immediately. Mike tried to ignore it, but Freddy's words "it's not good" stuck in his mind. Finally, he turned to his son. "Isaac, it's late. You should be in bed by now. I'll let you know what happens at breakfast." Eyes half closed, Isaac didn't argue.

Mike pried open his laptop again and stared at the image he didn't want to see. Was this really his daughter? No. It had to be someone who looked like her. Mike had seen people who looked just like someone he knew. That's probably what's happening here, he told himself. A lookalike, or … What was it? Oh yeah, a doppelgänger. That had to be it because his daughter wouldn't do this.

He pulled the laptop shut, turned off the TV and started upstairs. But what if she did? he asked himself as he slipped into bed, careful not to wake his wife. He wasn't sleepy. With wide eyes, he stared at the ceiling for what seemed like hours before losing consciousness. Throughout a restless night, the image on the website kept filling his mind. At six a.m. he was wide awake and exhausted. Before going downstairs, Mike checked on his phone for the final score of last night's game. "Figures," he moaned, shoving the phone into his back pocket.

"You got to bed late last night," remarked Cynthia, placing his toast on the kitchen counter.

"Yeah, the game went into overtime."

"Did the Leafs win?" asked Isaac.

Mike shook his head. "Maybe next time."

When Joannie dragged herself into the kitchen, she looked as worn out as Mike felt. Her backpack slipped to the floor as she took her place at the table.

"You look tired," said her mother. "When did you go to bed?"

"I lost track of the time, Mom. Amy and I were working on a project."

"Something for school?"

"Not exactly." Joannie grabbed a slice of toast. "I'm late," she said, and it seemed to Mike she was deliberately avoiding them.

Watching her leave, he echoed her words. "'Not exactly.' What do you think she meant by that?" he asked his wife.

Cynthia shrugged her shoulders. "I don't know. Maybe it was something sports related."

The image on the porn site flooded his mind. He raised a finger and stabbed the air. "Was Joannie out last night?"

"Whoa, Mike. She was in her room all evening. What's going on?"

He took a breath, trying to swallow words he wasn't ready to say. "Sorry, Cynthia. Look I gotta go too—inventory day."

"Hey chief," called one of his crew when Mike arrived at the warehouse. "Where do you want us to start the count?"

Mike gave him instructions before going to his office. He sat at his desk but accomplished little. Had he really seen a nude image of his sixteen-year-old daughter on that porn site? He practically jumped out of his skin when Freddy tapped him on the shoulder. "Sorry boss. You've been in a daze all morning. You ready for lunch?"

The two men chose their cafeteria food and found an empty table on the patio. Freddy broke the silence. "Did you look up that porn site? Is it her?"

"It can't be her. It must be someone else."

"Are you sure?"

Mike nodded, then shrugged. "Damn it, I don't know. I was awake most of the night."

"Why don't you ask her? She still lives with you, she's under your roof, you support her. Maybe it's just a teenage rebellion thing."

It was late and Mike was tired when he got home. Cynthia, Isaac and Joannie had cleared their dinner plates but were still at the table, talking.

"You must be starved, dear. I've kept your supper warm in the oven, so sit down and relax."

Mike grabbed a beer from the fridge and sat at the kitchen table, just as his wife placed the hot plate in front of him. Isaac asked to be excused, and stood up.

Mike hadn't intended to, but he turned on his daughter. "Joannie, someone told me about a picture of you on the internet. On a porn site. Did you know it was there?"

Isaac immediately sat back down.

"Dad, most of what you see on the internet isn't the truth. Everybody knows that."

"They do?" Mike didn't know that. The internet was his primary source of sports information. It was gospel. Why wouldn't the information be true? "So it wasn't you?"

Joannie frowned and looked at her father for a moment. "It wasn't all me."

Mike looked from Joannie to Cynthia and back to Joannie. "I don't understand."

"I don't either," said Cynthia. "Joannie, honey, what's going on?"

Joannie inhaled and flattened her hands on the table. "Okay, so there's this loser in my class. His name is Bruno. And like I said, he's a loser but he's also a computer nerd. And he's really good with Photoshop."

"Photo-what?" Mike interrupted.

"Never mind, Dad, that's not important. What is important is that Bruno decided to show off by photoshopping a picture of my head to a woman's nude body and posting it to a porn site. Why he picked me, I don't know, and I wouldn't have known about it except last night my best friend, Amy, phoned to tell me she'd read a tweet Bruno posted telling everyone what he'd done. Joannie looked at Mike and tears filled her eyes. "She sent me the link. It was awful and I felt terrible."

He felt a rush of fatherly protection and stood up. "What's this Bruno's last name. Do we have his phone number?"

Cynthia reached up to him. "Sit down, Mike. Let Joannie finish."

"It's okay, Dad. Yeah, it made me feel sick but then I got mad. I couldn't let that sexist pig Bruno do this to me without a fight. So I took care of it. I called Amy back and she and I figured out how to get Bruno to remove the image. That was the reason I was up so late."

Cynthia had been on the edge of her chair for the entire exchange. She leaned forward and asked, "And, what happened?"

"Bruno removed the image and tweeted an apology early this morning."

"I don't understand," Cynthia said. "How did you and Amy get him to do that?"

"Well, our first thought was to tell Dad. But he'd probably go to Bruno's house and, like, beat the shit out of him."

Mike nodded affirmatively.

"That didn't seem like a smart idea."

Mike shrugged.

"So what happened?" asked Cynthia.

"I'll show you what Amy and I dreamed up last night. Amy's a genius with graphic design." Joannie got her laptop and set it on the table. They gathered around the screen as an image came into view. Mike instantly understood how smart his daughter was. Cynthia was almost hysterical with laughter.

The screen displayed a colourful advertisement featuring the image of a gorgeous, muscled, six-pack body of a handsome young man with black curly hair. He was only wearing a thong and a come-hither smile. The headline read "Hi, I'm Bruno. Willing and ready. Looking for a long-term relationship exploring mutual sensuality." The words below the image read "Call 607-211-5400 NOW!" followed by a website address, GaySexFinder.com.

"Wow," said Mike. "Bruno must have received a ton of calls. How long did it take before he co-operated?"

Isaac squeezed in to get a better look at what everyone was laughing about.

"Dad, you've got to be kidding," said Joannie. "We didn't intend to publish this. As soon as we sent it to Bruno, he removed that image from the internet in, like, five minutes. The tweet went out early this morning."

"That is so good," said Cynthia, looking at the ad. "He's quite the hunk. What's the site again?"

Joannie looked at her mother. "Mom, you *do* know it's for gays."

Mike got up from his chair and put his arms around Joannie. "You're brilliant, Joannie. I'm so proud of you." He brushed away a tear.

Isaac looked at the three of them. "What's gay?"

Sharon Ramsay Curtis

LARRY, CURLY AND MOE 2005-2022
Celebrating the Wisdom of Keeping On!

I am a watercolour painter and often paint outside in all sorts of conditions. Wind and rain, insects and heat play a part in deciding how long and successful my *en plein air* sessions will be. As an outdoor painter my actions are sometimes of great interest to passersby, and many are very eager to find out what I am doing.

During the years that I have painted in public spaces, the most often asked question is, "How long did it take you to paint that picture?" It's an excellent question, but one that is very difficult to answer.

In June 2005, I retired from teaching kindergarten. As fall approached, when I would normally be returning to work, I luxuriated in the feeling of new things to do and experience. When my dear friend and painting partner, Martha Robinson, invited me to the Royal Winter Fair on one of the livestock days, I jumped at the chance. After an early morning breakfast and a trip from the country to Toronto, we joined the excitement of the Fair in the Stock Barn.

We settled ourselves in an aisle between some of the sheep pens and set to work trying to capture the essence of the animals before us. For me the day passed by in a blur. I was out of my comfort zone. It became apparent very quickly that it is one thing to paint a bucolic country scene and quite another to paint a constantly moving target.

The hustle and bustle of the crowds made our subjects very fidgety, and the arrival of pails of food made it necessary for us to take a break until the critters settled down for a postprandial nap. It was a wonderful day, tiring but very fulfilling. I had learned so much, but quickly realized that there was so much more to learn.

While we were working at the Royal, people often stopped to see what we were doing. To tell the truth, I felt like quite a bit of a fraud! Was I really an artist?

That session was the first time I had the courage to paint in public. It was a huge step.

I returned home excited to review my work. While I was proud of myself for getting out there, the results were less than stellar to my eye. It was easy to feel discouraged by the results, but I realized that I just needed to keep on making the effort and to focus on the process rather that the product.

Each time after that day I felt more comfortable. It became something I did more frequently.

Seventeen years later I found myself in search of much-needed space in my studio. I began to sort through old piles of work, and the forgotten paintings from the Royal came to light. Most were beyond redemption and went into the recycling.

However, there was one that seemed to have promise. It was a painting of the heads of three sheep, a Suffolk, a Leicester and a Romney. I set the painting up where I could see it, and gradually it began to speak to me. As soon as I knew what to do, I set to work.

All of a sudden, I realized the intervening years had given me painting skills I had not recognized. For a week, I spent time each day just looking and then adding touches that made all the difference. As I painted, I became quite fond of the three sheep and their little faces. I named them Larry, Curly and Moe. Finally, a voice in me said, "Sign it now. It is time. There is nothing more to do."

As this whole adventure was winding up, I realized that it is a great gift to be able to look back upon the things we do and to see a progression to excellence, no matter how imperceptibly slow. It is so important to recognize and honour that journey. The longer I live, the more I appreciate it. It is so important to keep on growing, and to trust in a positive outcome!

So, back to the original question, how long did it take me to paint Larry, Curly and Moe?

Is there an answer? Would you care to hazard a guess?

Kathryn MacDonald

SLANT
after Emily Dickinson

I
Dark rainclouds shade
a descending sun
force light low to earth
colouring
    boats and river
    trees along the shore,
    even swooping gulls
with unearthly hue
    deeper clearer truer
than the misty arc after rain
    its reflection and refraction
    its divine promise.

Tell the truth but tell it slant

When sunshine falls obliquely
details sharpen
    the heron's feathers lose
    the mottled cloak of mid-day
    each glistens silver-tipped,
    the small stones flat
    at noon now rise above
    long-cast shadows.

With this raking light we see
through the physicist's eye
   visible radiation
the poet's inner light.

The Truth must dazzle gradually

In this light what lies unseen
      flattened by sun's glare
      or hidden in dark shadows
breaches river's surface
stares eye-to-eye into
memory reimagined
a second chance to seek
surprise or *explanation*
perhaps to finally
whisper yesterday good-bye.

II
What of mystery
the divine light of slant

that opens eyes and channels
awakenings surprises

explanations to swallowed questions
those longings for touch

for sightings of the red-tailed hawk
love at the edge of woodland pond

rain on a tin roof
stories over dinner

scent of lilacs and peonies
birth in the paddock

spring of love born
and borne through years

mourning arrives too soon
this unknown a place to become

lost in light shadowed by dark
clouds slanted luminosity?

III
Listen for the moon's heartbeat.
Watch for her in the dusky sky
like a mirage taking shape.

Once you lay in her path
felt her cool breath on your skin
followed her out to sea.
She whispered lessons
of waxing and waning phases
repeating again and again
through awakening fullness / loss.
Sing through her rhythms.
They are ours.

Michael Croucher

OXFORD CIRCUS

It took a long time for me to stop thinking like a cop. To stop seeing the world like one. Friends told me I still walked and acted like a cop, always sitting with my back to the wall in a restaurant, watching the front door, sizing people up, ready for anything.

Many years after I'd left police work, something happened thousands of miles away from home that showed me things had changed. I had changed. That I could actually feel and show emotions. I was no longer an aloof peacekeeper and sometime enforcer who was ready for anything.

In the year 2000, I was on business in Europe, attending trade shows—one in Stockholm and another in Dublin. I had a few days between shows and decided to have another visit to the city of my boyhood: London, England.

It was a rainy Saturday. I spent three hours wandering around the Museum of London and was taking the tube back to my hotel near Victoria station. The underground was crammed with tourists and shoppers. I clutched a ceiling strap a few feet from a carriage doorway as the train rumbled into Oxford Circus, one of the busiest stations in the system. The carriage doors slid open. A new group of passengers wedged into whatever space they could find.

The last passenger to get through the door near me was a little boy of about six. He was decked out in a yellow rain slicker, yellow Wellingtons, and a yellow sou'wester-style hat. His rain gear was slick with moisture, the hat still dripping. He jumped through the doorway gleefully, landing with a thump on his shiny boots. His broad grin evaporated as soon as he turned back to the closed door and saw the faces of his panic-stricken parents on the other side of the glass. Understandably, the boy wailed. A man, probably his father, ran along beside the train as it moved away. He was yelling but his voice didn't penetrate the glass in the carriage doors. His message got through to a few passengers, because in an exaggerated way he mouthed the words, *next stop*. Quick thinking.

Two young ladies comforted the screaming boy. They were soon joined by a male passenger who identified himself as an off-duty London policeman. Together they took the boy off at the next stop, Green Park. They delivered him to a uniformed officer and a transit official, presumably to wait for the arrival of his parents on the next train. I imagine that was a joyful and somewhat tearful reunion.

When I got to my hotel room, I recorded the incident in a notebook while the memory of it was crisp. Note-taking is one policing habit that I will never give up. I'm a writer. Through those notes, images of what happened on the tube stayed with me for the rest of my visit to London. And beyond.

That incident at the Oxford Circus station really bothered me. I knew that the outcome could have been much different for that boy and his parents. The trauma could have been longer lasting, and more terrifying. Even tragic. During my eighteen-year police career, I'd seen horrific outcomes from little missteps or poor choices made by children. Yes, of course I'd felt sadness over such incidents, but I was never brought to tears. I never took the feelings home. On the job, most cops develop a detachment from these things. That detachment lets them go home after their shifts, likely still shaken, but able to get on with their lives.

For that little boy in trouble, things turned out well. He has likely long forgotten the incident. Even though I was simply an observer, I haven't. My reaction to what I saw signified that something had changed in me.

Back at the hotel, after I'd made my notes, I actually shed some tears. What the hell … was I having some kind of breakdown? I remember crying in my adult life only when my mother died, and to a lesser extent, my dad. And once when we had to put down our Wheaten Terrier. Those tears I'd kept hidden as best I could.

I still manage to keep my emotions mostly in check, but I'm no longer immune from having feelings, or showing them. To me, that incident in London served as a reminder. There are times and situations in life when we do misstep. Take a completely wrong turn, only to discover that we are hopelessly lost. Everyone has those moments.

I realize now, all these years later, that in my hotel room, I wasn't crying for the little boy on the tube. Not at all. I was crying for all those other kids, for other people. The ones who had truly tragic outcomes and for all the kids who were in the wrong place at the wrong time.

Janet Stobie

NIGHT TERROR

"Wilbur . . . Wilbur," she whispered.

In my dream, an angel reached out to me.

"Wilbur . . . Wilbur." The words were insistent, the whisper sharp.

I jerked awake. *What? . . . What? . . .* Silhouetted by the hall light, her white form glided toward me. My startled brain struggled to process what was happening. *Oh, no! It's Edna.*

There's no privacy in this place. Ever since they moved me into this nursing home, I have begged to have my door locked.

"Oh no, Mr. Tinklehurst," they keep saying. "It's not safe." *Now, she's come in the night. I have to get away.*

Her icy hand touched mine as she reached for my comforter.

"Edna . . . no . . . you can't . . ." My lips formed the words, but terror strangled my voice. I swung my trembling legs over the side of the bed. I could feel the cold emanating from her, as she slid in beside me.

"I . . . I've got to go . . ." I croaked.

"Hurry, Wilbur, hurry," she hissed as she snuggled down under my covers.

My searching fingers touched the softness of my robe, in its customary place at the foot of my bed. Awkwardly, I pulled it over my bony frame and shuffled forward, my bare feet clammy and sticking on the freezing tiles. Out in the hallway, my shaking hand grasped the handrail. *Hurry*, I thought. *I have to hurry.*

I peered ahead, searching for the night nurse. There, at the end of the hall, I could just make out her blurred form hunched over a chart.

"Help, help," I called, but still no sound passed my lips. *Keep going*, I told myself. *You'll make it.*

The nurse must have heard my steps, for she turned around and stared. Setting down her clipboard, she marched towards me.

"Mr. Tinklehurst, Mr. Tinklehurst, what are you doing out of bed?"

She loomed over my shrunken frame.

"It's ten o'clock. Everyone's asleep. Come now, I'll just tie your robe and we'll walk back to your room together."

I shook my head. My lips trembled. "No . . . No." The words refused to come out any louder than a whisper. "I . . ."

"Now, now Mr. Tinklehurst, you'll be just fine. You like your room. Your bed's got that cozy warm comforter your granddaughter made for you."

Totally ignoring my attempts to speak, she pulled my robe closed around me and tied the belt. "There now, that's better. Let's go." She took my arm firmly and turned me around.

"No, No." My hoarse whisper was louder this time. I yanked my arm away. "I . . . I'm . . ."

"Do you need to go to the bathroom? Is that what's wrong? Come along then, and we'll just take you there."

"No . . ." The sound exploded from my lips. "There's a . . ." My tongue felt like jelly. I couldn't form the words. *Speak, you idiot*, I commanded myself. Still no words came. I shook my head and tried to push the nurse away.

"What is it, Mr. Tinklehurst? You'll have to tell me. I can't read your mind."

She pulled on my arm. I could feel her frustration. My legs buckled. I pitched forward. My face landed in the middle of her ample bosom. In the midst of my distress, my mind registered, *at least she provides a soft landing.*

"Oh, I'm sorry, so sorry, Mr. Tinklehurst," she crooned, her voice full of remorse. She lowered me down onto a chair.

Tears of frustration poured down my face. *I have to make her understand.* "No, please," I whispered.

"What's wrong?" she asked, her tone once again compassionate. "You normally like your bed."

Another nurse appeared. "What happened?"

"Www … wwwoman," I mumbled and pointed.

Their eyes followed my shaking finger down the hall. Together, we watched the door to my room open. Edna Cortesi shuffled out, her wrinkled birthday suit revealed in the dim hall light. She stared back at us.

"Tinklehurst, what's the matter with you? Come here. I'm freezing," she shouted.

The second nurse abandoned me and hurried down the hall to Edna.

"Now, Edna dearie, let's go back to your room. We'll get your nightie on and wrap you in a nice warm blanket. You'll be just fine," the nurse said as she turned Edna around.

"Guess you've still got what it takes," my nurse whispered in my ear and helped me to my feet.

"Don't think I'll brag about being molested in the night by scrawny old Edna," I responded. This time my voice sounded normal. "Still, in the daylight and fully dressed, Edna looks pretty good."

We both chuckled.

Exhausted, I clutched her arm and shuffled back to my room.

Afterword

Over the years, I have been impressed by the resilience of many of the nursing home residents that I have visited. The transition from home to institutional living is difficult. The resilient Mr. Tinklehurst represents the struggle that many residents have with retaining their privacy while living behind the unlocked doors necessary for their safety. Sometimes the use of humour in presenting an issue can be effective.

Jessica Outram

THIS MORNING A MIRROR

I didn't see the bald eagle
nor the gulls or crows
in this awakening sky.

Just long grasses in this bay
still like a photograph
the absence of ducks or geese,
sway from a breeze.

Remember the black bears
strolling on this beach
chipmunks and woodpeckers
busy in the bush nearby.

Where is the deer
who stopped by this window
last summer?

It is so quiet now
without the hum of bees
or waves lulling on shore
this peace of stillness
welcome and worrisome.

Susan Dwyer

THE ACHE IN MY HEART

I opened my eyes. For a stomach-lurching second I couldn't figure out where I was, but then the familiar face of my doctor appeared over me.

"What did I have?" I croaked. My voice didn't sound like me.

"You had a boy," he replied softly, "but I'm afraid he didn't survive."

"Oh," I whispered. I shut my eyes and let myself fall back into the dark, where I didn't have to think about anything, where I could hide in my cocoon of sleep.

Sometime later I awoke again. I was in a private room. I was alone. I could hear muffled voices outside my door. I could smell something metallic. I swallowed and my throat felt as if an emery board had been rubbed back and forth on it. My tongue seemed to be sticking to the roof of my mouth. I coughed, which was a big mistake. Pain in my abdomen exploded and I let out a strangled cry, while trying to clutch my stomach. Coughing was definitely something to be avoided at all costs. My doctor's voice rose up in my consciousness. Had he told me my baby had died? Or was that some terrible nightmare?

The door opened, and to my relief, my husband Brian appeared at my side. He looked worse than I felt. I knew then that it had not been a bad dream. Our son was gone. He held me and we cried together.

This had been my second pregnancy. Our beautiful two-year-old daughter, Tracy, was at home with my in-laws. I ached to see her, to touch her, to breathe her into my soul.

For most of my pregnancy I'd felt ill. I'd wanted it over with, but like some cosmic joke, I went ten days over my due date. My doctor had sent me for X-rays; no ultrasounds at our cottage hospital in 1978. I was then scheduled to be induced.

It was called "being in the pits," as I was hooked up to a drip with Pitocin, a drug that was supposed to kick-start labour. However, my body must have missed the memo, because after hours of stopping and starting, my progress had been minimal.

My doctor had come into my room and beckoned to Brian, who had been sitting with me.

"Can I speak to you for a moment?" he asked rather curtly.

"Of course," replied Brian. He turned to me. "I'll be back in a minute." He squeezed my hand.

The "minute" stretched into what felt like hours and it was my doctor, not my husband, who returned.

"I'm sending you home," he announced. "The drip isn't working, although I imagine you'll go into labour this evening. That is what usually happens."

"Okay, thank you," I replied. Then for some reason I asked to see the X-rays. Deep down I knew something wasn't right and I wanted to see my baby. My doctor cleared his throat and refused to look directly at me.

"It isn't convenient right now," he muttered and left the room. I was surprised at his abruptness but reasoned he must be very busy with other patients.

The door opened. A nurse appeared, along with my husband. She began chatting and helped me get my clothes on. Brian was sent to get the car while the nurse pushed me in a wheelchair along the ugly grey painted hall to the front doors of the hospital. I vaguely registered that Brian's mood had changed and I didn't ask him what had taken so long for him to return.

The cold March air hit my face as I was pushed outside to the car. Within ten minutes I was back home and my beautiful Tracy flew into my arms. A moment of joy!

A week later I was still at home. No labour. The doctor scheduled me to be induced again. I was beginning to think there was definitely something wrong with me. My body wasn't working as it should. I knew if the induction didn't work this time, I'd have to have a Caesarean section, which was not something I wanted at all.

Hours went by with me "in the pits." Cramps would start, but if I moved, they would stop. The head nurse stayed with me all the time. I was getting so weary. I just wanted it to be over with. I was thirsty. I wanted to go home. Why wasn't my baby ready to be born? What was wrong with me? Suddenly, I felt a warm wet feeling down below.

"Oh!" I cried. "I think my water just broke!" The head nurse examined me carefully.

"Well, you've had a little bleed," she reported calmly, and put a pad underneath me. My doctor was summoned and then things moved quickly.

"We're going to do a C-section," explained my doctor. Another nurse appeared by my side. I was prepped and then found myself on a gurney hurtling along the corridor, pushed by someone definitely in a hurry to get to the operating room. I don't remember anything else until partly waking in the recovery room and hearing the devastating news that my baby had died. Later I was told that I had haemorrhaged, hence the race to the O.R. I also had five stitches and twelve clamps to add to my trauma.

It all seemed surreal, like watching myself in a movie. Even though Brian had confirmed the awful news, I felt a strange numbness in my soul.

A different doctor walked into my room and introduced himself as the coroner.

"Is there mental retardation in your family?" he asked abruptly.

The air seemed to leave the room. I couldn't process the question. Brian's face flushed with anger.

"No," said Brian, in a barely controlled voice. I don't recall the rest of the conversation. I shut my eyes and wished the man away. I longed to be back home with my darling little girl, and my husband, where I could forget this nightmare and be safe.

Later, my doctor came in to talk to me and Brian

"Your son was what we call anencephalic," he announced. "He had a brain stem, a chin, a nose and eyes, but no brain. He did not have much of a head." We couldn't speak. We were in complete shock.

"Did I do something to cause this?" I cried. My mind was reeling. *How does something like this happen?*

"We don't know exactly what causes it," he told me. He then said he had told Brian about our son's condition when I was first induced, but had instructed him not to tell me. He'd thought I would go into labour and be back that night and he didn't want me upset. Things hadn't worked out that way, and my poor husband had to bury his grief for a week, while I was at home unknowing.

The next day I was lying in my hospital bed looking out through a rain-splattered window at the grey sky. I could see birds flying back and forth on the bare branches of a giant maple tree, which was swaying in the breeze. The world was out there, still going along, just like every other day. Why hadn't it all stopped? My son had died. The world should have stopped.

My surreal feeling lasted for three days. I was fed, watered, cleaned up and made to get out of bed and walk, all the while feeling the pain of my incision and the ache in my breasts, as my milk came in. A very tight-fitting bra added to my discomfort, but the deeper pain went unacknowledged.

On the fourth morning, I was given my breakfast as usual. I removed the lid off the plate and stared at the shiny yellow glob that was supposed to be scrambled eggs. It smelled slightly of sulphur with a hint of antiseptic. I poked it with my fork. I felt I could squish it into a ball and bounce it across the room. A wave of anger came up from my gut, flooded my face, and I screamed.

"I can't eat this crap!" A tsunami of grief washed over me. Tears rolled down my face and splashed onto the glutinous mess on the plate. A nurse rushed into my room looking concerned.

"It's okay," she whispered, gathering me into her arms, "just cry it out, dear."

I howled. Great heaving wails were screamed into her shoulder and my tears soaked her blouse. She held me until I was exhausted, barely able to get my breath, then she tenderly cleaned my face, settled me back in bed and let me sleep. Later, when Brian arrived, I held onto him.

"I don't want any more children," I told him emphatically. "I couldn't bear to go through this heartbreak again."

Tracy was allowed to visit at some point. Someone had dressed her up with a nurse's cap, and my heart filled with joy to see her. However, she stood in the doorway with one hand on her hip, her chin up in the air, and glared at me.

"I'm mad at you!" she announced. My heart sank. I could feel tears threatening.

"Oh dear," I replied. "What's up?" I patted the bed. "Come sit next to Mummy. Just be careful of my tummy as it's a bit sore." She slowly came over and perched next to me. I wanted to hug her, smell her hair, feel her small body close to me, but I held back as I could see she was upset.

"You didn't come home," she said accusingly.

"I know," I admitted. "I wasn't well enough and the doctor wanted me to stay a little bit longer. I'm so sorry, love. Have you been missing me?"

"Yes," she said and several big tears rolled down her pink cheeks. I didn't know what she'd been told about the baby. I explained as simply as I could. How do you tell a two-year-old about death? I must have said the right things as she snuggled close and talked about home, her daddy and grandma and grandpa. It was so very hard to say goodbye to her.

"I'll be home soon, love," I said. She went with her daddy and waved goodbye. I felt utterly lost.

The next day when the nurses got me up walking, I decided to venture down the hall. I could hear a baby crying. "Please could I go and see the nursery?" I asked.

"Are you sure, dear?" The nurse looked worried.

Perhaps she thought I might have a meltdown if I saw the babies.

"I'm sure," I said. "If I don't go and look at the babies now, I might not be able to bear looking at one again."

The nurse held my arm and escorted me down the hall to the nursery. I was still a little wobbly and it was hard standing up straight with my incision still aching, but I was determined. I felt relief when I finally stood in front of the viewing window. All the babies were lying in their cots, swaddled in either pink or blue blankets. Most were sleeping but one was crying loudly.

"I think he must be hungry," I said, watching his face scrunch up and his mouth quiver as he voiced his displeasure at not being fed.

"He's a big boy who likes his milk," said the nurse, smiling to herself.

I took a big breath and let it out slowly.

I can do this, I thought. *I can get through this. I just need to go home, to my family. They need me.*

Several days later, I was allowed to go home. The head nurse sat with me for a few minutes, while Brian went to get the car. She took my hand in hers.

"I want you to go home and at some point ask your hubby to take your daughter out for an hour," she said. "Then go into the nursery, pack up all the baby clothes and have a jolly good cry."

"I will," I promised. We hugged. I was wheeled downstairs to my husband. I said my goodbyes and soon we were driving through the familiar streets toward home. Yet there was a strangeness to the world outside the hospital. It seemed too bright, too busy, too normal. My in-laws met me with warmth and love. Tracy clung to me, all smiles now that Mummy was back home.

I did pack up my baby's clothes. It was one of the hardest things to do. I also realized, as I neatly folded the clothes away in a box, that the really tough part would be meeting my friends and neighbours and seeing my sadness reflected in their faces. I came to realize that I didn't have time to grieve, not when there was a two-year-old vying for my attention. So I packed away my grief along with the clothes. Brian had to return to work, and my in-laws went home. My mother flew over from England and stayed for several weeks. It was "Stiff Upper Lip" time.

I kept putting one foot in front of the other. Brian and I went for genetic counselling, and to our relief, found I had only a six percent chance of another anencephalic child. It was not genetic. This fact helped me change my mind about more children.

In 1979, I became pregnant again. I took out the box of baby clothes I had packed away. I looked at the sleepers and the receiving blankets and felt that ache in my heart for the son I never got to know.

In December, I gave birth at the same cottage hospital. When my daughter was placed in my arms, that feeling of intense love overwhelmed me. In that moment, the ache fell away from my heart and joy burst in.

Melissa Thorne

ODE TO THE RESILIENCE OF A BUTTERFLY

burnt orange papyrus wings
dance amidst the waving wind
antithesis: fragile and robust things
missives the heavens temporarily exscind

embodying the souls of the dearly departed
weaving a skein between this world and the next
this nymphalid travels through realms uncharted
their message clear yet absent of superfluous text

the monarch epithet befitting the journey transcendent
though they do it without nation, crown, or throne
they twine a tapestry across a continent
to remind us we are not alone

Donna Wootton

WATER AND WOODS

ocean high rollers crash along the lake's sandy shore
giant roots and driftwood sit stranded making obstacles
easily bypassed when the water is low
now waves reach further inland

I remember when we explored the wild Pacific west coast.

snow settles lightly on evergreen boughs beside a narrow path
where dense forests of fallen logs are caught at awkward angles
easily trampled beneath overhanging branches
a ceiling under the sky

I remember when we hiked into Carmanah Valley to camp.

shades of blue reflect water depths
Caribbean turquoise
Georgian Bay cerulean
Mediterranean azure
Arctic Ocean indigo
all here at the lake where I walk alone
churning memories of a bygone life

Gwynn Scheltema

SING ON LITTLE SWALLOW

Andrew leaned his forehead against the cool window pane. Outside, driving rain rushed in off the ocean like beach sand blown against bare legs. Lightning and thunder came almost simultaneously now, confused and furious.

He tried focusing on single water drops on the glass; tried guessing how long they would resist the pull to the bottom; tried anticipating which would join with another and plunge headlong from their combined weight.

Shouts in the next room lashed at the wall like the rain.

He tried covering his ears with his hands, but his father's voice wormed in, garbled and distorted, as if he were lying submerged in the bathtub—snatches of phrases, odd words, like shattered glass.

As the thunder caught up with the lightning, his mother's voice shrilled like a caged bird. Words he didn't want to know, words he sensed would change things.

He imagined his mother a tiny swallow in the corner of a cage. He wanted to tell her not to panic, but she flapped and flailed, folded her forked tail, shivered her wings against the wire strands, blue-black feathers catching and holding her. Her rusty throat throbbed and her feet stumbled, upsetting food containers across the floor. He saw her cringe from the rough hand that reached in to grab her. *Wheet-wheet-wheet*, she cried. Over and over, *wheet-wheet-wheet*. Finally, he heard what he knew would come—the sound of hot urgent flesh against flesh.

When the thunder moved on, the red earth below the window ran like bloodied fingers over the uneven flagstone. Rain fell now only in gentle soothing drips from the trees. Outside, worms gasped in puddles. Beyond the garden wall, the pulse of the ocean called him. In the room next door, the swallow no longer trilled.

He fled the house by the back door, headed for the beach and the comfort of the mangroves. Here the swallows always gathered, and here on sunny days he liked to listen to their happy song as he lay among the dappled branches and watched clouds pass. But today, silence. No swallows. It was as if they had all disappeared, as if they might be angry at him for not helping his mother, his own wounded swallow.

His chest tightened and he gulped for air, felt the urgent need to untangle himself from the mangrove trees, head down to the wide, open expanse of grey ocean. Oblivious to the roots that might trip him, he stumbled down over the sand dune thick with knife-edged grass. Lead-legged, he plowed through loose beach sand towards the roiling surf. At the tide line, where the sand became firm and wet, he picked his way among hundreds of washed-up bluebottle jellyfish waiting for the tide. Above, seagulls dipped and swirled, pecking and clawing at the stranded feast.

Wind whipped whitecaps on the lagoon beside him, and on the far bank of the lagoon the marsh stretched towards distant dunes. Perhaps the swallows had gone there? Had they flown to the safety of straw-mud nests above the water? He needed to know. He needed to find them, make sure they had not gone away.

Sharp, slippery rocks across the lagoon mouth provided a place to cross to the marsh. Water funnelled furiously through the narrows, but he wasn't afraid; he knew these violent rocks. He also knew the tide was turning.

His throat was dry, and his breathing so laboured that his chest hurt, but he couldn't stop now.

Waves licked at his feet. The marooned blue bottles were beginning to float again. Salt air stung his eyes, coated his lips. He scrambled over the rocks, his feet slipping on their slickness, his palms torn on their jagged edges and limpet shells. On another day he would spend hours here exploring the world of rock pools, but not today. He needed to find his swallows; needed to know if they were okay.

Was everything his fault? Had he been bad? He'd tried to be good, but what if he'd done something that had made it all go wrong again? He coughed at the acrid smell of dead fish and seaweed. As he crested a rock, a sheet of ocean spray assaulted him, and he struggled to keep his footing. Waves sloshed over the rocks as if an invisible monster bird were taking a bath.

Jumping down from the last rock onto the marshland, mud squished between his toes. Behind him the tide waters surged into the lagoon mouth, red brown with churning silt. He knew if he stayed much longer, water would rise to several feet over the rocks, and the current would be too strong for him to return to the beach.

Spread before him, the marsh reeds waved back and forth with the swells, their feet trapped in the mud. He couldn't see any nests, nor a single swallow. He thought again of his own swallow. He'd wanted to help her so many times before, to save her, but always fear had stopped him. This time he would be brave. He must go farther, find the swallows.

Taking a deep breath, he pulled his sinking foot from the silt and stepped forward. But the water was deeper than expected, and a buffeting wave washed away his balance, crashing him sideways into the broil. Sand churned at his thighs, its coarse fingers probing his flesh. The current sucked him under. Open-fingered, he raked the water to no effect. He tasted gulps of gritty salt water, felt the alternate swells of warm and cold currents snake around him. Stones and shells sliced his feet, and when he opened his eyes, he was yards from where he'd stepped in.

With each stroke he swallowed salt and sand, and felt the pain of brine forced through his nose. He cut out blindly for the mangroves across the lagoon—all he could see above the waterline. His arms were heavy and difficult to lift above the water, but when he tried breaststroke, his body sank deeper into the fury. He kicked his legs as hard as he could, his body tossed like a stick, the undertow pulling him with every stroke.

Finally, the water grew calmer, and his groping hands grabbed fistfuls of silty slime. He dropped his feet to test for the bottom, and felt them touch tangles of seagrass roots, spongy and oozing through his toes. The plants were just visible above the water now, as he waded chin deep among them, feeling the brush of plankton and darting fish and other things he couldn't identify. Emerging from the wet, the matted greenery became sand beneath his feet, and he flopped exhausted on the dry, shelly surface, still coughing.

The beach was deserted, except for a lone fisherman on the point at the other end of the bay. Andrew wanted to be that fisherman. Untroubled. His tears came like the rain had done. Was his swallow gone forever now? He had tried to be brave and failed. Was it all his fault?

Andrew looked towards the mangroves, knew he must get up and go home, face what he had been unable to prevent. But his legs were jelly, so he drew them up beneath him, dropped his forehead to his knees and waited for strength.

Soon the wind subsided and the calm returned. Then chirping in the mangroves made him lift his head and listen. Swallows. The swallows were back. They had survived the storm.

He took a deep breath and stood up. Turning from a sea washed in the pinks and mauves and yellows of the sunset, he started for home.

Kim Aubrey

FIRST OF DECEMBER

Crow in the road crunches salt
crystal an incisor-like seed.
Snow encrusts fallen leaves,
empty twigs and fence tips.

Dream I keep to my bed
while daughters chatter and feast
in the next room, dissecting
platters of appetizers.

I am not so much sick as inert
a gas that's seeped away from the world.
Blanket's green field spreads toe to chin,
sheet a white band fastens my chest.

Before the snow I cut the last roses,
buds' spiked heads, set them in warm water.
They keep summer's scent—honey and fruit.
One relaxes a bit, loosens its collar.

My morning class sweeps snow from green grass.
We dance on slick brown leaves and seed heads.
Their stems bow. We shed toques and coats,
unfurl. Sun warms our faces.

Arms like a wave we summon geese
from the sky. Arms an arc of light
we cast off despair, chew the cold,
swallow it, turn air into energy.

Later clouds have reclaimed the sky
and everything has melted,
the rose buds droop on the sill.
Soon winter will begin again.

Robert Pearson

TOUCH

Felt her heart beat
in the palm of my hand
caressed her scare
felt her tension
as I gazed at her loss
Kissing her eye lids
She eased at my touch.

Marie Arden Prins

THE GOLDEN FORTUNE COOKIES

"Aww man! Not another stupid, boring party!" said Jordie, smacking his forehead when his mother broke the news about their New Year's Eve plans. No friends. No cousins. No aunts or uncles. Just Mom and Dad, Gran and Poppa. Like last year. Same old bubble. Jordie wanted to stab that balloon of a word. Toss its torn pieces in the trash. He was so done with staying home all the time.

"We'll make pizza," Gran promised. "Watch a movie. Eat popcorn."

Poppa winked at him. "Can't be too awful, son."

Jordie scowled. Maybe not for old people. But totally unfair for him.

At least they had shopped for his favourite pizza toppings—mounds of mozzarella cheese, pepperoni, bacon, green olives and pineapple bits. Gran had even made her homemade pizza sauce. Its spicy aroma tickled Jordie's nose. By suppertime, his stomach rumbled. Grudgingly, he covered the harvest table with bowls of chopped food, balls of sticky dough, round pans, spoons and brushes.

Gran supervised the flattening and pinching and stretching of dough. Mom oversaw slathering the sauce and spreading the toppings. Poppa manned the oven, while Dad gathered the drinks. One by one, the personal pizzas were baked and devoured. Jordie took his last bite just as Gran's bubbly pizza was slipped onto her plate.

"Better than store-bought!" said Poppa, leaning back in his chair. He didn't seem to care that half the toppings had slid off his crust and a few stuck to his flannel shirt.

Yeah, maybe, thought Jordie. At least better than the school lunch ones that skimped on pepperoni. "What's next?" he asked. His expectations were low.

"A full stomach makes me sleepy," said Poppa. "I think I'll go to bed."

"No way!" Jordie protested. "It's not even ten o'clock!"

Mom stood up. "Let's clean the kitchen and do a jigsaw puzzle." Jordie groaned. Dad laughed. "Tell you what, let's watch a movie on Netflix while your mother searches for identical, tiny pieces." Jordie shrugged. He wished he could play Minecraft, but he had used up all his iPad time that afternoon.

With a drawn-out sigh Jordie haphazardly piled plates on the counter until Gran shooed him out of the kitchen. "Poppa can help me wash the pans," she said. "It's too early for his bedtime."

Jordie dragged himself into the living room, plopped on the sofa, and watched his mother sort puzzle pieces on the card table. Just as his father started their movie search on Netflix, the doorbell rang.

"Who can that be so late?" Mom asked.

Dad went to check and returned with a box wrapped in shiny red paper and topped with a handwritten note from the Golden Fortune Cookie Factory: "May the New Year bring you Joy."

Everyone denied ordering the cookies or even knowing the factory's whereabouts. Dad wondered if an out-of-town friend had sent them. Mom thought maybe the family of one of her elderly patients had them delivered anonymously. But no matter, they crowded around the box and opened its lid. Inside, five crispy fortune cookies nestled in their wrappers.

"A perfect treat after a full meal," said Gran.

Jordie's hand shot out to choose one, but his mother reminded him that grandparents chose first. Poppa playfully nudged him. Then he picked the middle cookie, cracked it open, and read his fortune. "An inch of time is an inch of gold."

"Well," he chuckled, "at my age, all time is gold."

Mom chose next because Gran's hands were in the dishpan. "A golden egg of opportunity falls into your lap this month."

"More gold! Hope that's true," she said. "It's been a tough two years."

Dad picked next. "All the efforts you are making will ultimately pay off."

"Couldn't ask for a better fortune!" He popped the cookie into his mouth.

"Go ahead, Jordie," said Gran. "My hands are still wet."

Jordie stared at the two remaining cookies. Geez, not much choice.

He read his fortune. "A feather in the hand is better than a bird in the air."

"Seriously? What does that mean?"

Dad shrugged, but Poppa offered, "I think it means that it's better to have a feather than something that flies away."

"Who wants a feather? That's a dumb fortune." Jordie tossed the cookie pieces back into the box.

Gran raised her eyebrow, but said nothing as she picked up the last cookie. "A golden future awaits you."

"Well, that sounds promising," she laughed. "We've had enough worries this year."

"Listen!" exclaimed Dad. "I hear fireworks! Bet it's the guys next door."

They bundled into coats, hats and gloves and rushed outside. Streaks of red, blue and green shot into the dark sky. Whoops and whistles and shouts of "More! More!" echoed from the neighbours gathered on porches and driveways. Caught up in the excitement, Jordie hollered along with everyone until he was hoarse. But when the display was over, his neighbours retreated indoors. Jordie remembered other New Year's Eve parties when he and his cousins had run around the yard waving sparklers until midnight. Then everyone had hugged, slapped backs and wished each other a Happy New Year. Right up close.

Epic fail this year, he thought as lights winked out around the neighbourhood.

He followed his father into the house. "Hey Dad, let's watch that movie now."

His father yawned. "Don't you think it's rather late for a movie?"

No, he did not. If his cousins were sleeping over, they'd watch movies all night in the basement rec room. His family was a bunch of old fogies. He squinted daggers at his father.

"Go brush your teeth," Mom said as she wiped the counter.

"Good idea, son. We're all heading for bed." At Gran's request, Dad slid open the deck door and dumped the dish pan over the railing so its doughy water wouldn't clog the drain.

Jordie scowled, stomped upstairs and banged his bedroom door shut. He didn't care that Poppa was already in bed. And he wasn't going to brush his teeth. Who'd notice pizza stuck to them? No one. That's who. No one.

When Jordie woke in the morning, a weak sun shone through his window. Frost sparkled on the glass, promising a cold day trapped inside with his family. He squeezed his eyes shut and prayed they'd let him play video games all day. But probably not. He'd get stuck doing that impossible puzzle with his Mom and Gran. So he waited until his stomach demanded breakfast before he headed to the kitchen, where four grim faces greeted him.

"What's up?" he asked warily.

Poppa sighed. "Gran lost her wedding ring."

"It was covered with dough, so I put it on the windowsill by the sink." Gran's eyes were red. "Now I can't find it. We've looked everywhere."

"Some golden future," muttered Mom. Dad promised to search again after breakfast was finished.

Wanting to escape the worries inside the kitchen, Jordie quickly ate his cereal and pulled on his coat. It might be a new year, but it felt just like the old one. Grumpy people inside his house. And everyone else isolating in their own homes. Again.

He headed to the backyard shed to retrieve his hockey stick and net. At least he could take shots in the driveway. But the net was jammed behind the lawnmower and his bike. He grabbed his stick and swung at the icicles hanging from the roof. They plunged with satisfying cracks into the snow. He retrieved a large one and brandished it at a low-hanging spruce branch. A shower of snow fell on his head and neck. He jumped sideways and slipped on an icy patch.

For a moment Jordie lay still in the snow before rolling onto his back. Above, the sun peeked out from behind thin clouds. *Keeet. Keeet. Keeet.* Two blue jays, perched high in the tree, called to each other. Jordie liked their harsh sounds. Sort of how he felt inside, loud and screechy. *Keeet. Keeet. Keeet,* he mimicked. They flew away and he grinned.

Then a chickadee, plus another, lighted onto a limb above his head. *Chick-a-dee-dee-dee.* They flitted from branch to branch, cheerily tilting their black caps this way and that. *We know you're here and it's okay,* they sang. Jordie watched them until the cold seeped through his clothes and he shivered. As soon as he stood up the birds scattered. He shook himself and felt pleasantly lighter, as if a trouble or two had winged away.

Nearby he spotted a double line of bird tracks in the snow. They led towards the lilac tree by the house. When he followed them, his saw something bright in a bare spot by the deck. A blue feather. He reached down for it and a glint caught his eye. A golden glint under bits of pizza crust and a thin sheet of scummy ice. He cracked it with his boot. There was Gran's ring. As he slipped it on his finger, the blue jay landed on a lilac branch, bobbed its head at him, and flew up to meet its mate. Jordie watched them soar over the roof. Then holding the feather, he hurried into the house to tell his Gran that her fortune had come true. And, if he played his feather right, a golden day of video games would land in his hands.

James Ronson

HOPE

Shelagh stands by the window and gazes out at the waves crashing upon the huge masses of rock, snow and ice. Sancho is poised by the plate glass window, anxious to be out. Sancho, the dirty brown fluff-ball, who looks and feels like a shag rug from the early days of the Sixties. Shelagh's is a peripatetic life but Sancho loves these moments. There are trails and laneways and one-way streets everywhere in town. The dog is a blessing, especially during COVID-19, when all are confined to barracks.

There are some days when she leaves him home. *Sorry Sancho, I'm sketching and photographing today.* When Shelagh sets out on her own, she studies and sketches the interplay of light and waves, the vermilion and coral light when the sun strikes the clouds, the chaotic confusion of patterns of leafy greens and tangled tree masses in the reflections on the rippling waters of the creek, the greening yellow bullrushes guarding the marsh where the swans nest.

She is following in the footsteps of a favourite artist, J. M. W. Turner. He took to the countryside *en plein air* and inspired a whole medley of French impressionists to do the same. Back in her studio to the rear of the cottage, Shelagh transforms these moments into stirring paintings, multicoloured abstract textured works with layer upon layer of trowelled, sponged and feathered compositions.

Today, she and Sancho must stay put. A dire snowstorm has descended upon the town. Whiteouts prevail. The vulpine wind whirls about the cottage and a blizzard subsumes the aether. Woman and dog are stuck inside the house as the snow mounts, layer upon layer, blocking both doors, papering the lower half of the great bay window, threatening to bury all beneath its relentless, implacable onslaught.

Shelagh lies restless and awake, listening for the sound of snowplows or at least a train whistle. The baying wind and the crashing surf are all she hears. Living so far from town, she knows hers is one of the last roads to be plowed. Complicating matters, Ricky, the guy who always shovelled out her walkway and the driveway, died of a heart attack in January. She had hoped to get through the winter without finding someone else to aid with the load. Nothing to be done now but try and succumb to sleep.

She awakes to a room too cold and too dark. There must be a power outage. It's freezing but she needs to use the washroom. Shelagh slides her legs across the bed and sits on the edge, searching with her feet for her slippers.

How will she ever find her way to the bathroom in the dead of night? Usually, she can rely on the flashlight icon her daughter had pointed out on her cellphone, but the battery is too low since an earlier talk with Lil. Worried about the storm, her anxious daughter had wanted her to spend the night in a hotel.

Oh, don't be ridiculous, Lil. I'll be fine. Would those words come back to haunt her? How long could she last in this frozen tomb by the lake?

Giving up on the slippers, Shelagh fumbles for her robe, finds it at last, and wraps herself up against the cold. Next, she slides by Sancho, who is whining and wide awake now, sensing something is wrong. Slowly she extends her hands in the darkness and reaches out for the bureau. She can use it as a guide to cross the room to the doorknob. Lil's words about the cottage purchase come back to haunt her: "You'll be miles away with only that damn dog to help you. And why would you even consider buying a house without an ensuite? You know, Mother, you're up at least once a night to use the bathroom."

I'll be fine, Lil, you just watch and see. Shelagh fumbles for the doorknob, finds it, and slides it open. She uses her hand to feel her way towards the bathroom, her feet shuffling down the hallway on the new hardwood; she'd had the carpet ripped out due to static. *I could use the sparks from the static electricity to help me see right now. Then again, maybe not.*

Sancho's tail swishes in the hallway. From the bathroom, Shelagh trundles into the living room in search of any vestige of light, her dog by her side. Outside all is snow and darkness, black against white, white against black.

Not a single light is visible. The whole town must be out. Not even the flashing amber of the solar powered lighthouse is visible in the driving snow, and there is no sign of dawn.

Her teeth are chattering. *Come on, Shelagh. Think! Where will you be warmest?* The art room with the skylights is always the coldest room in the cottage. The next coldest is her own bedroom. She decides the best place to wait out the night is on the chesterfield in the living room. She can bundle herself beneath the quilts and invite Sancho up for mutual warmth. She settles onto the couch and pulls Sancho up beside her. Eventually, she feels the sleep waves washing over her.

When she shivers awake, a nacreous pallor is visible through the bay window. Is dawn finally here? Has she survived the night? Has the snow finally stopped? She yanks the quilts from her body and in the feeble light succeeds in reaching the front door. She tears the door open to reveal a veritable wall of snow. It covers half the door frame. *Hell, that's a lot of snow. How can I possibly escape?* There's no telling when the lights will go back on. This sheet-white mountain is all she can see beneath the dull grey skyline. Even the snow volcanoes that have formed along the beach remain invisible behind the amorphous mass of white.

Shelagh hears Sancho stirring behind her, growling at the wind and snow. What about Sancho? She remembers the delight the dog takes in snow-jumping acrobatics. *I'll bet he could do it.*

Shelagh finds the flashlight on the hook near the door. "Come on, Sancho, follow me."

He shadows her into the bedroom. She disrobes and puts on her street clothes. Retrieving her backpack from the closet, she throws her dead cell phone, her charger, her mask and her wallet into the pack. No time for niceties like purses. She sets the backpack down beside her and puts on her boots and her outer winter clothes.

Next, she extracts a broom from the front hall closet and opens the door to an icy blast of air off the lake. Undaunted, she thrusts the broom out into the snowbank. Wham. Layer by layer she whisks the snow away until a simulacrum of snow steps appears in the wall blown up against the front of the house.

"All right Sancho, it's your turn." Shelagh closes the door, takes up his harness and attaches the leash. "Up, Sancho! Up!" she urges, and takes her first step up the incline. Sancho lunges up the bank. "Steady now, boy. Wait. Okay, up Sancho up." There is a pull on the leash. One, two steps more. At last, she reaches the top of the bank. "Wait." He glances at her but remains still. "Good dog." Slowly now, she steps down the bank, her boots half buried in the snow. Finally, they're free. "Okay Sancho. Let's go."

Sancho continues to pull gently on the harness and Shelagh follows his paw-printed path through the snow. It is a long, exhausting trek but they make it out to the expanse of snow covering the main road. The willows, coated in hoarfrost, wave their feathery arms in the wind off the lake.

How 'bout this damned dog now, Lil?

She looks back to look at her cottage. Years ago, Shelagh fell in love with the title of one of Turner's poems, "Fallacious Hope." For her cottage, she'd hand-painted the words on a sign to provoke the curiosity of guests and passersby. Now she sees that the sign has become dislodged by the storm. *Fallacious Hope*—hanging by a threadbare wire.

Finding tire tracks made by her neighbour Gus, Shelagh and Sancho get in the groove. She can follow this route along the road by the lake and then head north past the river and the factory into town. Roads, cars and gardens are buried in snow. No movement is visible anywhere. The Port is a deserted ghost town spirited away by the snow.

Shelagh trudges on behind Sancho and at long last reaches her goal. Her friend Naomi runs a boutique hotel in town. As with all the businesses during the pandemic, Naomi's hotel is closed to the public, but Shelagh is hopeful Naomi will let her in. She puts on her mask.

A light shows inside, reminding her that Naomi has a generator. She steps through the door and feels almost blinded by the light.

"I'm sorry ma'am, the hotel is closed to visitors. And you certainly can't bring that dog in!"

"Naomi, it's me, Shelagh!"

"Oh, it *is* you."

Both hesitate with the indecision that the plague carries about hugs. "What the hell," says the maskless Naomi. She runs up to Shelagh and throws her arms around the neck of her friend.

As they sit to enjoy a hot cup of coffee, Shelagh says, "You know that art show I'm hoping to have at the gallery in town? I believe I have a name for it. I plan to call it 'Energy and Light.' The latter is a nod to Turner and the past, and the former is all about our present century. After all, finding alternative sources of power will be paramount in the coming years."

Naomi tosses her a wry grin. "Yes, Professor Wright."

"Okay, Naomi, pardon the donnish lecture. Now, where was I? Oh yes. My paintings and Sancho. Let's not forget him. I fully intend to picture him in a composition called *Tilting at Wind Turbines*. That ball of fur may have saved my life last night."

Robert Pearson

BELLY AND BONE

Winter settled in
all round
Chilled to the bone
Day light struggles
Against the dark
Air is still, frozen
Branches motionless
Beasts and fowl
Retreat into the glens and forest
Sun lies low below
The treetops
Sky turning
Lemon to
  Butter Yellow to
      a Rose Blush
All into the Steel Blue nite sky
Barbecue futile
Frozen air defeats
The heat
Fireside and silence
Fragrance of soup wafts through out
Warms the belly and bone

Al Seymour

THE BEST SLED RIDE EVER!

It was 1962 and just two weeks until Christmas. For the thirty-two kids in the combined Grades Three, Four and Five class at Cook's School, we should have been excited. But we were not. We were grumps.

The first snow of winter had not yet arrived. We were so very tired of the brown dead grass and the brown mud-filled roads. The sky was grey every day—rain and cloud, cloud and rain.

We lived in Creighton Heights, a neighbourhood in the country that was filled with big hills, ponds, creeks, forests and fields to explore and enjoy. We lived for outside play, and in winter—skating, tobogganing, pond hockey, snow forts and snowball fights. But this winter, there was nothing to do outside. Winter with no snow? Not fair!

Monday morning was our arithmetic test. Double not fair! With my bright yellow pencil in my right hand, I chewed new teeth marks into the upper end, ready to begin the times-table test. On Mrs. Bowman's instruction, we turned the purple ditto test paper over. I sniffed the paper. Alcohol—the stinky test paper smell—went right up my nose.

All right. Seven-times table—begin! I quickly completed the table up to eighty-four, followed by the eight-times table to ninety-six. Done. I sighed in relief. I could smell the wet wool of hats and sweaters hanging at the back of the class, the dusty chalk from the green board. And Danny Brown, sitting in the Grade Four row beside me. Sometimes he smelled, and today was one of those days.

Looking up from my desk, I checked out the class. Everyone was still figuring and writing. The class was quiet except for Sandy in front of me, snuffling with her cold, Danny's sister Jessie shuffling her feet, and Alex in the Grade Four row tapping his pencil. On the walls and windows were crooked, class-made snowflakes and Christmas wreaths of green construction paper with red tissue paper hollies held on by thick gobs of mucilage. I glanced at Danny Brown. He had dried blood on his sleeve and on his freckled cheek was a big welt the size of a fist. *Ricky!* Ricky the bully from Grade Eight was always picking on Danny. Then someone farted. Giggles erupted.

"Class!" said Mrs. Bowman loudly. I pretended to be still writing the test. Then, from the corner of my eye, I spotted it.

Outside, one ginormous snowflake fell slowly, waving at me as it floated back and forth, past the windows, towards the ground. Then another and another. Ten—twenty—fifty!

"Psst, Eric," I whispered. "It's snowing."

My best friend Eric sat across the aisle and one seat up from me. He dragged his fingers through his straight black hair, then started to chew his shirt collar. He hadn't finished the test.

"Eric," I said a little louder.

"No talking!" boomed Mrs. Bowman.

I hid from her gaze, my chin on the desk. "Sandy, it's snowing!" I whispered to the pale girl with stringy blonde hair who sat in front of me.

"I said no talking!" boomed Mrs. Bowman again.

I looked up. She was standing right in front of me. She was tall, with grey curled hair. Her horn-rimmed glasses hung on a small chain about her neck. Her red lipstick looked like she had kissed a candy apple. She always wore the same sweater over her shoulders, even when seated at her desk. She was old, and sometimes she was mean.

She stood with her hand on my shoulder, until all the class had completed the test, until each student had put hands together neatly on the desk. I was sweating and I couldn't move. But she could not stop the excitement that was building. The whispering grew louder. Giggles were heard from a number of kids in the class. Fingers pointed, eyes stared, and grins widened. *Tobogganing, sledding and sliding after school!*

"Yes, yes, it's just snowflakes," said Mrs. Bowman, taking her hand off my shoulder, as she announced, "Test over." I looked up at her and she winked at me.

The snow became so thick that the whole outside world looked white. It was like a monster dump truck in the clouds was trying to cover up the school. The three-thirty bell finally sounded and we were released.

We wore the latest winter fashions: wool toques, leather hunting caps with woolly ear flaps, leather or knit mitts, rubber boots, leather boots, coats done up tight and coats undone showing their plaid flannel liners. Susie had her snowsuit buttoned up to her armpits, and because it was too tight, she walked like a penguin. Jane had her toque pulled down and scarf pulled up, revealing only her eyes. A tuft of red hair was the only way to tell it was her. I pulled my Maple Leaf blue-and-white toque down tight, then zipped up my navy-blue nylon coat with red-checked flannel liner. Two layers of my mother's knit mitts covered my hands. Snow boots and a pair of long johns under my blue jeans completed my snow gear.

The Browns only had hand-me-downs from older brothers and sisters: hulking, stained green corduroy coats with ripped pockets spilling wool batting, pants with patches, and toques and mitts with holes.

Down the school hill, over the creek bridge and up the opposite hill by the Bartons' house, we slogged through the deep snow. Toboggans, sleds, and racers were pulled from garages and summer hiding places.

I followed Eric to the top of Barton's Hill, then put down my wooden racer. The skinny luge-like sled had wood slats nailed over two wooden runners. Two polished steel rods were attached to the wood runners. It was light and it was fast. "Ready!" I yelled.

Eric placed his four-seater toboggan down on the soft snow, pull rope in hand to prevent it from sliding down the hill on its own. "Ready!"

The twins, red-haired Susie and Jane, prepared their Canadian Tire "Flyer" sled with steering bar, steel runners, and wood slats, set high off the snow. Back and forth they pushed the sled to create a starting track. "Ready!"

The Browns, Jessie in Grade Three and her brother Danny, had only a sheet of cardboard.

"Go!" yelled Eric, as he jumped on board his toboggan. It did not move. He began pushing with his hands. The toboggan still would not move. I rushed to help him, pushing his shoulders. The toboggan moved, but only inches. It sank deeper into the soft wet snow.

My racer would not budge. It was like millions of tiny snowflake hands were grabbing the runners and all calling out, "No!"

The twins' sled would not move either, stuck in the track. And the Browns' cardboard sheet? It just got wet. We gave up, defeated, and sadly pulled our snow craft home. The deep wet snow had won.

The next day was sunny and colder. The school bell rang at three-thirty. We were off again. Today we brought our snow craft to school so as not to lose sledding time. Turning to look behind as I crossed the creek bridge, I noticed Ricky from Grade Eight and two other big boys closely trailing Danny Brown. The big boys had armloads of snowballs.

On Barton's Hill, the deep snow was just a little sticky—good for making snowmen.

Eric settled onto his toboggan. He pushed with both hands, using all his strength. The toboggan inched forward. Stuck. Alex and I pulled and pushed, eventually making a packed toboggan run all the way down the hill. After her first slide, Sandy walked up the hill in the new track and Alex reminded her of hill rules—no walking on the course. Sandy glared back at him, sticking out her tongue. Danny and Jessie arrived late.

The Browns lived on Garden Street. The houses there were small with wooden siding, not brick, and often not well kept. Some had car parts lying on the lawn. Those of us who lived on other roads looked down on the Garden Street kids. Garden Street was poor street.

Danny and Jessie placed their cardboard sheet on the hill. Down they slid, slowly. First frontwards, then backwards, sliding off the course into the deep snow, but only halfway to the bottom. We laughed at both of them.

Wednesday was mild, and by lunchtime it had started to rain. The course looked ruined.

On the way to school Thursday morning, I met Eric at the top of Barton's Hill. Despite a coating of sand, a car was spinning on the road. Its tires whined, and its back end swerved as it tried to make the top of the hill. Eric looked at me with a wide grin. Ice!

We climbed over the fence to inspect the toboggan run. I lost my balance and fell, sliding down the run on my nylon coat. Eric dropped into a squat, racing on his boots like a runaway brick on two feet.

Our class was full of noise—all day. Mrs. Bowman put on her mean face, trying without success for quiet.

Back on the hill at four o'clock, it seemed the whole school was ready to slide. Today, my racer was super-fast. Going down the run headfirst, I bumped with each depression, my chin only inches from the ice. The twins' sled was super-fast too. Jane steered and both girls shifted their weight to do small turns. Toboggans lost control, some sliding sideways, some backwards, some dumping their riders. The cardboard sheets spun out of control, then ripped. Danny and Jessie walked their ripped cardboard up the hill, as Ricky arrived with the two other boys from Grade Eight.

The three laughed at the Browns, calling them names, making sure everyone knew they were not welcome and that they should go back to Garden Street where they belonged.

Danny and Jessie, heads down, quickly departed.

On Friday when we arrived on the hill after school, we saw something new. Halfway down the hill was a jump. A big one made of icy packed snow. Danny stood at the top of the hill, waiting, his arms crossed. He seemed different. Had he made the jump?

Eric lined up his toboggan, and with Alex aboard, quickly took off. The toboggan veered sideways and hit the jump crooked before flipping over. I sat on my racer, hit the jump and was thrown into the air. The racer continued riderless to the bottom of the hill, while I smacked down, right on my butt.

Jessie appeared from behind a tree pulling a new thick cardboard sheet. Danny turned it over to reveal an iced bottom. "Check this out," he said. "Made the ice at home."

He and Jessie ran together then jumped on top of the cardboard, racing face first toward the jump. The cardboard and riders leapt into the air, way up, then thumped down, continuing far into the valley. We just watched. *Whoa!*

Saturday was cold and sunny, and by mid-morning the hill was full of kids. Alex came with a cardboard sheet, flopping down on the run, then spinning wildly. Eric too had a cardboard sheet, which he shared with me. We spun out of control. Half the kids had cardboard. We went one after another on our wildly wobbling whirligigs, sliding in all directions. Then we all locked arms for a massive group slide, ending in a pile of snowsuits, cardboard sheets and laughter.

When we returned to the top, Ricky and his two friends had arrived without sleds and without cardboard. Ricky first taunted Alex, calling him poor. Then he turned to Eric, pointing at him and his cardboard sheet. Where were Danny and Jessie? I spotted them pulling a massive packing case over the fence.

Danny and Jessie moved with purpose, ignoring the rude comments from Ricky and his friends. Setting the box on the course, Danny asked for help holding the box to keep it from sliding. No one responded. I looked at Ricky and the two other big kids, then at Danny.

Danny only looked at me and my friends. I tugged Eric's sleeve, indicating we should steady the box.

Ricky moved to block our path. I looked up at the black mop of hair on top of his pimply face. I didn't blink. I took a deep breath, then brushed by him, followed by Eric. Eric and I braced the box, as Danny and Jessie got in. Ricky moved to block the box's path. He sneered, facing the box riders, then the rest of us. Danny and Jessie were tense, gripping the box edges tightly.

Alex walked past the two big boys. "We need pushers!" Susie, Jane and three others quickly brushed past the big boys, positioning themselves behind the box—hands outstretched, ready. Jessie, her eyes fixed on Ricky, raised her fist and yelled, "Let's do it!" Eric and I leapt aside as the pushers shoved.

The box sped up quickly, heading right at Ricky. Just as I thought Ricky was going to knock Danny and Jessie over, he jumped away. The riders zoomed down the hill. Just before the jump, the cardboard turned and they hit the jump going backwards.

"Whoooee!" Jessie and Danny threw their hands up in the air. The box rocketed down—way down into the valley.

Everyone on the hill had stopped to watch. That was the fastest ride and farthest distance ever down Barton's Hill. Danny and Jessie were grinning as they marched back up to the hilltop.

"Good going, Jessie!" yelled Susie.

"Great ride!" called out Eric.

I clapped my hands, the twins and others did too. The big kids shut up, even Ricky.

And as we cheered, Ricky and the two big kids left the hill. Jessie looked at me with a big grin, a grin I had never bothered to see before. Her pigtails were sticking out of her red wool toque. Her leather mitts were wet, her snow pants patched, and her coat was two sizes too big. But it was her smile on that freckled face. That was for me. I clapped again.

She pointed to me and then to the unoccupied cardboard box and nodded. I climbed in, Jessie and Eric followed. Danny, Jane and Alex pushed as hard as they could.

We moved so fast. We hit the jump right in the centre. Up, up, up. "Whoooee!"

That was the best sled ride ever.

Kathryn MacDonald

THE SHEDDING

...the tree
knows what it takes to shed everything. Randy Lundy

I have come to this island
to shed everything dry and brittle
   the grief carried a decade and more
   old skin and habit.

I have come to lose memory
of peonies dropping red petals,
the house wren nesting in the arbour,
the garden pond   its rippling waterfall
where your tuxedo birds came to bathe
when berries ripened on prickly brambles,
the empty Adirondack chair.

I have come to shed yearning
   the weight of whispered words.

I have come to feel my soles sink into the sea,
for the ocean to scour bone's marrow
with the healing of salt and sand
rubbed into the wounds of mourning.

Through the sea's ebb and flow I am learning
the lessons of the waves' breaking   their crescendo
   each slow withdrawal making way for the next
making way for what's next

                  making way...

Heather Beveridge

ISLAND SURVIVAL

Mary Hannah stopped, dropped her head into her hands. It was all she could do to stay awake but she was desperate to do so. The fire in the stove had to be stoked, or the family could freeze. She worked on her sewing to keep awake, and when she finished sewing the last button on Jack's overcoat, she draped it over a chair and moved it closer to the hot stove to dry. *Thank God he fought for his life. We can't survive without him.*

She'd worried, as she always did, when Jack had set out for town across the icy lake, but their situation was dire and they needed supplies. He had started later in the day, expecting the ice would freeze solid and the bright moon and stars would reflect on the snow and light his way home.

Their oldest girls, Jane and Alice, had helped Jack harness the horses to the big sled they used for carrying logs and building supplies. Mary Hannah had watched from the window as he carefully led the horses down onto the ice. Jack climbed on the sled, waved and was away.

The girls were just getting ready for bed when they heard someone calling. It was Jack climbing up the path from the lake—no horses in sight and his clothes were frozen to his body.

Getting Jack's wet clothes off him quickly had been a challenge. The girls pulled off his heavy boots and socks while Mary Hannah cut the buttons from his coat with a knife. Jack's teeth chattered and he rubbed his arms for warmth as he explained what had happened. "The team was travelling along fine. The ice was smooth and the sled glided well, when suddenly a dark hole appeared in front of us. There was no warning. The horses made it over the hole but the heavy sled started to drop into the water. I jumped from the sled," Jack said, tears filling his eyes. "But I couldn't save the horses. The sled pulled them under. There was a ghastly scream. I'll never forget it. Their terror echoed and then there was an eerie quiet."

The horses—it was a terrible loss but Jack was safe. Mary Hannah coaxed him into bed with the hot water bottle and a mustard plaster to ward off any cold or chills. As much as she felt like crying, Mary Hannah smothered her tears. *I must keep strong for the girls.*

By the light of the lantern, Mary Hannah reflected on how she had come to this dark and snowbound place in northern Ontario. It was not how she had expected her life to be while growing up in Yorkshire.

***

She had just finished her weaving when her Great Aunt Ruth found her on the staircase.

"A letter has come for you, Mary Hannah! It's not from Lizzetta; it's not the same hand." Mary Hannah thanked her aunt and sat down on the step. Ruth leaned on the newel post and waited. Mary Hannah began to read aloud slowly.

Dear Miss Wood,

I trust this letter finds you well. Your friend, Lizzetta Boothroyd, has advised me to write to you and ask for your hand in marriage. Lizzetta is a dear friend of mine and my deceased wife, Ellen. With great sadness, Ellen left this earth on Valentine's Day leaving me with a lovely baby, Caroline Valentine, who is two.

Caroline's grandparents, Ellen's mother and father, are looking after her for me. I desperately need someone to look after Carrie as the grandparents will not be able to continue much longer.

Please consider coming to Canada if only at first as a nursemaid. However, if you find me to be a suitable candidate, I would be prepared to marry you. I have enclosed the money for your passage to Canada but I have also enclosed enough for your return trip if you find that I am unsuitable as a husband.

Lizzetta tells me that you are a good woman who will make an excellent mother and wife since you have had experience growing up with a large family.

I've enclosed a letter from Lizzetta to you as a reference to my character. I sincerely hope that you will take my proposal seriously. I look forward to meeting you.

You can write to the return address and let me know when you have made arrangements to come.

With my utmost love and affection,

Your servant,

John (Jack) Hopper

"Well, imagine that," laughed Aunt Ruth. "Would you actually go all the way to Canada when you don't even know the man or his circumstances? What if he turns out to be a drunk? What if you don't like him?"

"I might," said Mary Hannah. "He's a friend of Lizzie's and she's included a note with his letter."

Lizzetta Dawson, Mary Hannah's best friend from school, had written every few months since she had moved to Canada. She had sent a letter when she married Fred Boothroyd and another when Fred was killed in an awful train wreck in Toronto. Now poor Lizzetta was pregnant and had two small boys.

Dear Mary,

I've asked Jack to include this note in with his letter to you. I suggested he write to you. Jack Hopper and his wife Ellen have been so kind. They made sure that the boys and I were being looked after throughout that unexpected tragedy when Fred was killed.

Jack's wife Ellen had the consumption for a couple of years and died when Carrie was two. Carrie's a beautiful little girl but Jack's not the best at looking after little ones especially with him working at odd hours for the city.

I know it seems strange but I know that Jack will make a good husband and father. He works very hard as a teamster and handyman and has a good home. He doesn't drink and he and Ellen had a very happy marriage.

If you can come it will be so good to see you and to have a friend by my side.

Love, Lizzetta

Mary Hannah wanted to go to Canada. She missed her friend and she knew what it was like to lose a mother. She had experience looking after children, thanks to the brood her stepmother brought into the family, and little Carrie needed a mother. She could trust Lizzetta. If her friend vouched for Jack, she was sure he must be a good man.

***

Mary Hannah had made her decision, and fifteen years later she had four beautiful daughters and Carrie was grown with a baby of her own. She looked into the bedroom and saw that Jack was sleeping soundly. He had such a scare and was so upset about the loss of the horses. He loved them almost as if they were family, and these two, hand-picked by Colonel Talon, were a lovely matched pair.

Now, what were they going to do? The question kept going around in her head without any answers. There were four little girls to feed and Christmas was coming. Another reason for Jack's trip was to surprise the girls with something nice for Christmas. Now there was no way off the island.

In the coming days, Mary Hannah kept them fed with soup made from vegetables left in the root cellar. Soon there were no eggs or milk and the flour was almost gone.

They could walk across to the mainland if the ice would freeze hard. Mary Hannah wrapped her shawl around her and huddled into the rocking chair. She would try and use the wood sparingly. Jack was slowly regaining his strength but she didn't know when he would be fit enough to cut more wood.

As she rocked, Mary Hannah began to knit. Ideas were floating around in her head. What could she make the girls for Christmas? Perhaps little dolls from some of her fabric scraps, and she could also make lace. She worked into the night, eventually falling asleep in the chair.

She woke with a start as she heard the girls in the loft. Luckily, the fire had not gone out and she used it to make their last bit of porridge. Before the girls came downstairs she heard a voice.

"Hello! Hello!" A voice in the wilderness? No, it must have been the wind in the trees. No, there it was again.

"Girls! Come quickly," she called. "I think someone's at the dock."

As they scrambled down the path to the dock, they could see the top of his hat and gradually the figure of Harry grew as tall as a ten-year-old boy could.

"Harry! Harry! We're so glad to see you. How did you get here in a boat?"

The young lad from across the lake had rowed and pushed his way through the ice. "I haven't much time! Mama thought you would need these things—there's flour, eggs, butter, milk and some vegetables from the cold cellar."

"Your mother was right. This is wonderful. We would have starved. The horses and the sled went through the ice." Everyone was trying to talk at once.

Young Harry lifted the sacks onto the dock. "It's already looking stormy. I have to get back before everything freezes up, but I'll come again in a few days."

They stood on the dock and watched the small figure in the wooden boat as he half rowed and half pushed the small craft across the ice and the open water. Before Harry came, Mary Hannah had been able to make soup, but there was not enough flour for another loaf of bread. Now, she had best get started.

Within a few days, Jack was up and around and able to meet Harry at the dock, tell him his story and thank him profusely. "I have a letter here for Colonel Talon. Can you put it inside your coat and get your Mama to send it down to Toronto for me? I need him to know what happened. Our family won't be doing this again."

Colonel Talon,
Queen's Park Av.,
Toronto, Ontario
Dear Sir;
It is with deep regret that I have to advise you that my family and I will be leaving Chief's Island as soon as the first boat arrives in the spring. It has been a terrible winter. The ice would not stay frozen making it impossible to cross to the mainland for food.

I attempted to cross one night when I thought the ice would be solid. I very much regret however, that there was open water that couldn't be seen. The horses although they made it across were pulled under the ice by the heavy sled and have been lost.

Fortunately, I was able to jump from the sled in time and not get pulled under. I made my way back to the house and the family has been stranded here since. If it was not for Mrs. Waters' son coming with a boat across the ice and open water we would have starved.

I understand from the stories I was told by the Waters family that my family was not the first family to be left on the island in the wintertime. I am upset by your negligence in not informing us of the possibility of being stranded. For that reason, my wife and I will be leaving your employ once we are able to leave the island.

I would ask that you continue to pay us for our time on the island especially considering the hardships that we have endured with our small children. Much of the work on the new cottage has been completed and I expect to be paid for that work.

Wishing you and your family the best for a good Christmas.
Yours sincerely,
Jack Hopper

Leaving the island on the first grocery boat in the spring, Jack, Mary Hannah and their girls took the train to Toronto. Jack got his family to safety but only lived one more year.

("Island Survival" is based on the experiences of the author's ancestors during the winter of 1902 on Chief's Island, Lake Joseph in Muskoka, Ontario.)

Pam Royl

WHAT SHE LEARNED

The brilliant sunshine reflects off the freshly groomed snow. Jane should be listening to her twenty-something ski instructor, Todd, explain the rudiments of skiing. But his stunning blue eyes are putting her on edge.

They're standing on top of the deceptively steep bunny hill at Sunshine Village resort in Banff, Alberta, surrounded by a deafening squad of small children. Jane feels like the Wicked Witch of the West amongst the Munchkins. A few of the tiny demons display an easy aptitude for skiing. Others throw tantrums, terrified at the prospect of harnessing gravity—these are her people. She'd even made the mistake of dressing like them: bulky ski pants, heavy jacket, and the yellow helmet she'd chosen—thinking it was cute. Jane's mood is darkening at the absurdity of it all.

It had been her friend's idea to try skiing. "Do something outside your comfort zone," she'd said, then promptly abandoned her when the day came for the first lesson. Something came up, apparently. Jane intends to "unfriend" Vicky at the first opportunity. How would skiing make her feel better about her fractured life? Staring down the steep hill at the chaos of tiny figures webbing randomly across it, she contemplates an escape route that doesn't require the use of skis.

"We'll start with a basic lesson," said Todd.

Basic is what she needs, but as he begins, Jane pays more attention to him than his words. He radiates the confidence only good-looking men possess. Life must be easy for Todd. But she wonders why he isn't smiling.

Todd flexes his muscled body, spreads his arms and says, "Imagine you're hugging someone." He glances again at the attractive female blonde ski instructor he's been flirting with since the beginning of the lesson. It's becoming obvious to Jane that Todd is more interested in his love life than in paying customers. Finally, he refocuses, points the tips of his skis together and separates the tails away from each other. "Put your skis like this. It's called the snowplow position." He enunciates the last two words as if she were a small child or an addled senior.

Jane struggles to follow his direction, but when one ski starts to slide, she ends up on her ass. Her face is burning and sweat runs down her spine. Rather than offering help, Todd's attention wanders back to the pretty instructor. After a few fumbles, Jane manages to get the skis beneath her and plants her poles. She crouches and pulls up, panting and red faced. About to crash to the ground again, she steadies herself, smiling at the accomplishment "Now what?" she demands of Todd.

He shrugs. "Watch," he tells her and slides down the hill about ten metres, maintaining the snowplow position. He then stops and waits, but he's not watching how she begins the descent. Instead, his eyes search behind her—undoubtedly looking for that pretty blonde.

Taking a deep breath, Jane assumes the correct stance and starts down the slope, mimicking his movements, her thigh muscles screaming all the way. It feels as if she is in a full-body clench. Feeling like a stuffed scarecrow, she laughs, and loses her balance but with determination makes a wobbly recovery. She stops awkwardly next to Todd and grins—it is more of a smirk. She refuses to let his inattention spoil her small victory.

They continue down the bunny hill, with no further instruction from Todd. When they reach the bottom, he makes an announcement. "Okay. Time to go up the lift."

"What? Up there?" she says, gesturing toward the mountain with its summit smothered by clouds. Her legs begin to tremble.

Ignoring her protest, he glides gracefully toward the loading area of the lift. "Follow me," he yells over his shoulder, not looking back to see if she does.

She glowers at his back. Maybe she should cut her losses and write off the lesson as a failed experiment. Then she remembers a different blue-eyed man who walked away from her. Emboldened by the memory, she scrambles after Todd like some bizarre lizard—refusing to give up.

Stopping in the lift lineup under a sign announcing *Strawberry Express Quad*, Todd nods stiffly when she reaches him. Swallowing the knot in her throat, she nods back. Waiting their turn, she watches the fully loaded chairs sweep up and away. Behind them, the lift line begins to grow longer. Fighting to keep steady, Jane envisions the chair hitting her, sending her tumbling, the eager skiers gaping at her sprawled on the ground. Jane startles when Todd suddenly pushes her forward before she has time to prepare.

"Oh, Okay . . ." She scrambles to position her uncooperative skis on the mark Todd has made by tapping the tip of his pole. Suddenly, the chair catches the back of her knees, drops her into a sitting position and starts moving up the mountain. "OHHH." Stomach sinking, her skis now dangle in the air. As gravity threatens to suck them from her boots, she leans forward.

"Watch out!" Todd yells, grabbing her sleeve. Jane presses her back against the chair as he lowers a safety bar over her head to rest just above their laps.

Gripping it fiercely, she takes a deep breath, then settles in and is surprisingly captivated by the spectacular view. Snow-dappled pine trees sparkle at the borders of the ski runs, with graceful skiers snaking underneath as the chairs ascend the steep face of the mountain. Lost in the view, she relaxes against the hard seat. Her mouth spreads into the first genuine smile of the morning. She has no sense of the time it takes to reach the top.

Todd remains silent and Jane considers protesting his lack of instruction but decides to remain quiet when she notices his distant gaze and the tension around his eyes. As the top of the lift rapidly approaches, Jane says, "Ah, Todd, you do realize I have no idea how to get off this thing, don't you?" A nervous giggle rushes out of her mouth followed immediately by a choked gasp.

He turns slowly, as if he just remembered she is sitting beside him. "Okay, stand up when your skis hit snow."

As their unloading approaches, Jane watches the skiers ahead, hoping for more guidance. When each chair reaches the top, the skiers stand effortlessly and glide down a gentle slope. She envisions her own graceful landing, but her momentary confidence is shattered when Todd yells, "Keep your tips up."

With her skis about to embed themselves into the snow as their chair lowers, Jane struggles to raise the tips, finally feeling the reassuring impact of packed snow beneath her skis. She stands but immediately crashes down on the offloading ramp, unable to get up.

"Move or you'll stop the lift," Todd yells, before seizing both her arms and pulling her out of the way.

Once vertical, she shakes off his hands and fumes. "You should have told me about holding up my tips earlier. It threw me off," she snaps louder than intended. Her helmet suddenly feels too tight, and she senses everyone's eyes on her.

With a sigh, Todd leads her to the top of the so-called easy green run. She shuffles along behind him and wonders why she's paying good money for this non-lesson.

When they reach the top of the run, she gulps for air. A dense white mist covers the slope. Skiers start down the run, immediately disappearing within the thick haze. Todd plants his poles in the snow and leans forward as if desperate to see the bottom of the hill. Jane is about to ask what he's doing, when without one word of instruction or encouragement, he vanishes down the mountain.

Jane plunges her poles deeply into the packed snow to keep herself from sliding. Her heart pounds and she casts around looking for help. No other instructors are nearby. Slowing her breath by inhaling deeply a few times, she watches confident skiers start down. Each one takes a noticeable angle to the pitch of the slope, cutting across it horizontally instead of straight down. She gingerly repositions her tips.

"Don't let fear stop you now. You've been through much worse," she murmurs softly to herself. Cautiously she nudges forward, remembering to form a snowplow at the last minute. Air rushes past her helmet as she plummets into the mist. Everything disappears and she's floating within a cloud, while blindly sliding downwards. Ahead, the bright green jacket of a skier—stopped on the side—emerges through the mist. A gentle rise slows Jane's momentum, and she surprises herself by stopping easily beside the skier. The woman nods and says, "Nice stop."

Full of gratitude for this small encouragement, Jane smiles and watches the woman descend the next slope. She starts to follow when suddenly a man races past, his skis spraying her with snow. He comes so close to hitting her, Jane falls—hard. Pain rushes up the hip that lands on the hard-packed snow. "Sh … Sugar!" she yells. Snow covers her goggles, sweat pours out every pore. Her injured hip throbs. She could let her threatening tears flow, but Jane knows self-pity has never helped.

Summoning courage, she stands. Her skis slide forward and she follows the path of the green-clad woman. By crisscrossing the steepest slopes, cruising over the flatter sections, and stopping frequently to plan her next move, Jane makes it down the mountain. When she reaches the ski racks, she sighs with relief and looks up the mountain she has just conquered. "Who needs *Todd!*" she says loudly.

Suddenly Jane is famished. A few minutes later, she sits at a table in the restaurant, devouring a hamburger, while she considers demanding a refund from the ski school. Todd should not have abandoned her like that. It was unprofessional.

Sipping a cola, Jane spies her incompetent teacher huddled at a corner table with that same female instructor. It's surprising how different he looks with his helmet off. His blue eyes are dark, and he seems vulnerable, less self-assured. His features remain strong but his face is drawn and the corners of his mouth drop in a sad frown. The woman is petite, tanned, and sexy in her slim ski pants and tight sweater. But her shoulders are shaking, and she is wiping her eyes. The way he gently kisses her hand, then wipes a tear off her cheek, suggests an unexpected tenderness. Jane recognizes something familiar in their body language and she can't stop staring at them, completely aware that it is terribly wrong to be so curious about strangers.

Her tears dried, the young woman pushes her chair, tenderly kissing Todd before turning to leave. He reaches for her. She pauses to squeeze his hand, then lets go and walks away. Todd lowers his head into his hands and pulls at his hair.

Jane turns away. A moment later, a rustling sound draws her attention. She looks up to see Todd standing beside her table. His face collapsed around his sad mouth.

"Jane, I'm sorry. I shouldn't have left you."

She remains silent.

"Look. I can give you a refund." His lower lip trembles slightly and his chin quivers.

"Are you afraid I'll get you fired?"

"No. that's not it." His voice breaks.

Jane points to the chair across from her. "Please sit. What's wrong?"

He hesitates then says, "Listen, this may be out of line, but . . ." When she nods encouragement, he goes on. "I saw you staring."

Her face flushes. "I didn't mean to pry—"

"That's my wife, Sally . . . Well . . . she got some bad news from the doctor's office this morning."

"So that is why you were so distracted."

"I couldn't think of anything else. It's breast cancer," Todd blurts out.

Jane realizes what their body language was telling her.

Todd looks around nervously. "God, I shouldn't be talking to you about my problems."

"Listen . . . I had breast cancer."

His eyes meet hers. "Oh shit. Are you okay?"

"Well, I'm here, aren't I? Learning to ski on my own!"

He looks down at his clasped hands. "I gotta say. You are one tough lady. I don't know what I was thinking leaving you up there like that."

"It's hard to think at all when you first hear the word *cancer*."

They sit in silence for a long moment while Jane decides. "Here's my advice. Take it one step at a time. But Todd. Don't run away from her."

He sits back, his eyes wide. "I would never do that." He pauses for moment. "Wait. Do you think because of what happened on the mountain today, that it's my thing to just, just ... leave?"

"My fiancé did."

Todd stares, then says, "That is just ... horrible."

Jane nods. "Right after I was diagnosed. But I found a strength I didn't know I had. I am not going to lie. The treatment can be rough. The side effects are awful. It's a club that no woman asks to join, but once you are part of the community, we support each other."

"Thanks. Sally would like that."

Jane pauses. "And Todd, I want to thank you too."

"What? Why?"

"It was wrong to abandon me. But I got down the mountain. I did it on my own. I plunged into that mist just as I did with my treatment. It was ... reaffirming."

"Glad something good came out of it. But I'm still refunding your lesson."

Jane reaches into a pocket for her business card. "Here's my number—if Sally ever wants to talk to someone. You know, who's been there."

He stares down at Jane's number as if it held magic.

Katie Hoogendam

Q&A/ROI

Snow like tufts of milkweed
on this, the last day of winter.
My sister texts to say she's emailed
about our other sister's remains.
Remains. What a word.
I had just completed a very complicated
conversation with an Investments Specialist
at the bank. After taxes, I had a little left over.
I had planned to meet in person
but stayed home instead to nurse
our eighteen-year-old dog, who is dying.
His warm head was in my lap while I attempted
to decipher the difference between risks:
low and high, conservative, aggressive.
And what did I want to invest in?
The bank lady prodded me, my cell
balanced atop a mason jar atop the kitchen table
above me, where my dog and I lay on the floor.
My dog yelped, seized, relaxed. He hasn't eaten in days.
The bank lady waited courteously
for my answer.
What will we do with his remains?
I asked her.

*"Return On Investments": metric to calculate the profitability of one's
investments.

Antony Di Nardo

THOUGHTS ROBUST WHILE SITTING OUT THE PANDEMIC OF '21

I yearn for the day Amazon will return all the money I've given them
(no amount of blushing will change what they owe me)

I left the embrace of wilderness for the teat of consumption long ago
The elixir of every whim I've had continues to trickle down my throat

All my life, aisle after aisle, I fed myself on comfort, needs and
acquisition
I deserve my tool box and the purpose that it serves when empty

Back and forth, back and forth those are my people at the trough
I find winter foliage at its best when the trees are bare

It's giving back all I've taken that's disconcerting
Resistance like resilience is another word for keeping up my spirits.

Wally Keeler

POT SMOKING IN BLAND LAND

POEMPEII, Poetency Press: Several units of verse of the universe of the glorious Imagine Nation of the Peoples Republic of Poetry (PRP) were arrested in Bland Land early yesterday evening on charges of possession of poet for the purpose of trafficking and being intoxicatingly eloquent on poet in a public place.

The units of verse had been touring Bland Land as part of a shoutreach program, known in poetry circles and triangles as "Give the Bland a Hand." The program had been developed by the Creative Intelligence Anarchy in collaboration with the Federal Bureau of Inspiration.

The units of verse admitted to being poet smokers. They were reportedly in possession of an undeclared quantity of "Onomatopoezia: sans simile," a genre of poet that condenses the imagination to its primal routes; grunt, groan, moan alone along on long lines of sound slam.

Proseph Stalin, Motivational Director of the Bland Gland Brigades, announced the arrest: "Bland Land has come under direct assault by the 101st Word Warriors of the Imagine Nation of the PRP once too often. It is done under the cover of poetry readings, spoken word performances, slam funk poetry or other sub verse euphemisms, all with the purpose of overthrowing mediocrity, the stabilizing governing principle of Bland Land.

"These misguided units of verse were found to have Pure Poet in their possession. Studies have found that chronic poet smoking, principally by those of the most delicate sensibility and the most enlarged imagine nation produces a state of mind that is 'at war with every base desire' as one of their poetic revolutionaries once put it."

The Minister with Poetfolio of the PRP, condemned the charges. "Poet smoking is nothing more than the inhalation of airy somethings to rearrange the local habitation and names of their origin allies. It stimulates the central inspiration system. Let's be blunt. Bland Land is a verbless noun. They are seriously blandicapped.

"To arrest and detain our units of verse is nothing more than blanditry. We appeal to the United Imagine Nations to demand the release of the creative forces that through the green muse spurts worlds of multiconceptualism."

The Creative Intelligence Anarchy released a terse statement: "Poet smoking is the leading cause of flights of fancy free. The Imagine Nation will not be grounded by the farces of the S.O.R.E. virus (Suppression, Oppression, Repression of Expression). We will continue to enforce landing writes in the blandemic wasteland of mediocrity. Those units of verse will not be ablandoned"

***

Muse Update: Poets found free early this morning at 5 a.m. Eastern Stanza Time on the write side of the border, away from Bland Land. They are currently debriefing in Poettsburgh, Poemsylvania. The leader of the Poemaceutical Performance Poets said they had been motivated by Irving Layton's credo, "Whatever else, poetry is freedom."

Poetician1 declared, "Freedom is worth all the blood it takes to prevail. Poet smoking is the write of every unit of verse of the glorious Imagine Nation of the Peoples Republic of Poetry. Long Live Write Supremacy!"

Alan Langford

MANIFEST LIFESPAN

Roger wasn't sure when it made the transition from a hypothesis to belief, or when it went from belief to faith. Whenever it was, he regretted it as deeply as any thought he'd ever had. No matter. For a few more moments, here he was.

Very long ago, maybe in his forties, Roger observed that most people had no real expectation for their lifespan. When their time was up, it was up. *C'est la vie*. But others were different. Some set clear expectations. Early on they aimed to live until they were thirty, fifty, ninety, even one hundred. Roger started to notice that a lot of people who set their expectations came very close to meeting them. Certainly not everyone. Some were victims of mishap, some lived longer, sometimes far longer than they had expected. But many who truly believed that they'd live to a particular age often came very close to doing so.

This dovetailed with how Roger saw others live their lives. These people feared death but they never tried to negotiate with it. They lived, filled their lives with the moment, played the cards they were dealt, didn't give it much of a second thought. By and large they all seemed happy, except perhaps at the very end.

Then there were the "intentionalists"—the *Think and Grow Rich* types. Noting that most successful people had the intention to be successful, they falsely inverted the logic, concluding that intention was all that was required for success. They did not grasp that while intention is necessary, it is not sufficient. Unable to accept that if two people were competing for the same prize, and if both had been equally dedicated to manifesting a future where they won that prize, at the end there was still precisely one prize. The universe simply did not split into two and allow both to win.

Yet in defiance of this logic, odds did seem to favour those who had the greatest fervour in their intention. While universes did not bifurcate to meet every deeply held desire, imagining the future somehow had influence over the general direction of future events. Roger had once heard a Zen sensei say, "Imagine a future of war, and you will get war. Imagine a future of peace, and you will get peace." The only hypothesis that fit was that the universe was in fact some sort of grand simulation— in effect, a game where collective expectation could alter future realities.

By the time he was in his fifties, this was Roger's truth. Many expectations for his life had already held true. He wanted two children, a boy and a girl. He got two girls—one transitioned. He wanted a great love, and he had one, although ultimately it rendered his heart in shards. As he reassembled the pieces, he wished for a gentler love and he found that in Carol.

Roger came to believe that if life really was a simulation, then some external force had to be operating it, much like playing a game. Never much of a theist, he hypothesized a society where unknown intelligent beings lived a very long time, thousands or even millions of his years. A place where a human lifespan would be a blink, like playing an old arcade game. What he saw as fifty years of an uneven life could be a brief moment for this intelligence in a universe that he might never become aware of. He thought of that consciousness, ready to casually evaluate his life and either hit the "play again" button or move to the next form of entertainment. He imagined a console emblazoned "Life on Earth, twenty-five cents per play, three plays for fifty."

If this hypothesis held, he could change the game play merely by setting an intention and elevating it to a belief. Even though age was starting to set in uncomfortably, life had been acceptably good so far. The thing to do was to decide to live longer. Much longer but not forever. Forever had been tried a hundred million times and had never worked.

Roger decided he wanted to live to be two hundred and fifty years of age.

That was his fateful hypothesis. Over time he stuck to it. He repeated it to himself. He told his friends. When he heard of someone reaching an age of one hundred and ten, he'd say they were a hundred and forty years short. He said it so many times that he came to believe it. In time, it developed into a deep faith.

At first, there were genetic approaches. New treatments repaired telomeres, greatly slowing the aging process. Then freshly cloned organs, cures for most cancers, therapies to keep brains healthy, and bionics were perfected. Innovation upon innovation. These things let Roger live a healthy life, well past one hundred, as they did for many others. Researchers talked about extending human lifespan past two hundred. Like the monk had said, people had imagined a future. In this future people lived to two hundred and beyond, and the universe was delivering a reality to fit.

Many imagined living longer, but too few imagined the circumstances of that longevity. At least too few to change the future. At a hundred and thirty-seven years old, facing an ever-decaying ecosystem, Roger, Carol, and about two hundred and fifty others, including some of his children, grandchildren, and great-grandchildren, moved to a self-sustaining community. Deep underground, it drew its energy from geothermal sources. There, they hoped to weather the factors that were rapidly making the Earth's surface uninhabitable.

It was always a long shot. Maybe not enough of the group believed with the intensity required to have it manifest. One year, a virus mutated. Virulent, it killed almost half of them. Cruelly, this included all of his descendants. The catastrophe overwhelmed Carol. She struggled for years, then took her own life. Roger fought for her every day, but his hope and belief was shy of faith. Insufficient.

The years, the decades, slipped by. A variety of fates befell the rest of the community. Accident and illness, be it physical or mental, took them all. All but Roger. He carried on diligently, monitoring the surface for life.

It remained deadly.

As the underground pod's self-repairing systems reused parts and shut down unused sectors, they still provided food, water, and all the essentials in steady supply. Time passed unabated. Various automated systems marked its passage. They reported on surface conditions and attempted to entertain with games. He read, meditated and hoped. He exercised less than he should. He struggled to retain language; if he ever managed to return to the surface and encountered another remnant of civilization, he wanted a chance of communicating.

One day he awoke to an alarm. This wasn't too unusual. Another system had gone offline. Likely some self-repairing switch had self-repaired for the last time and needed manual replacement. Not a welcome way to wake up, but better than the usual monotony.

As it happened, this time it was different. The only remaining gas exchanger was failing and irreparable. In a matter of several days, the pod's environment would degrade to the point where life wasn't sustainable. This was an expected, virtually inevitable, end for Roger. He'd long since accepted that the chances of safe return to the surface, toxic for over a century now, were almost nil.

But still he longed to see the horizon, to take in the curvature of the Earth. Roger decided to have a last look. It took two full days to prepare. Rigging a pressure suit with spare parts, diverting some of the gas exchanger's failing capacity to produce mere hours of breathable compressed air, practising getting his withered, tired limbs into the suit, and testing it. He was exhausted.

Even knowing this was his last night, he slept well. He wondered if his theory of this life as a simulation was right. Would he know or even find Carol and his children in the place he might return to? Or was it all disposable game play? How miserable was life in this hypothetical universe if the painful struggle on Earth was light entertainment? Was it this thought that finally emerged as fear of death?

The next day Roger woke early, hours before the pod's artificial sunrise. He ate for no particular reason and began the tedious process of suiting up, testing systems that he knew would last at best half a day before he fell into a final oxygen-deprived sleep.

Tests completed, he climbed the long ladder to the first lock, opened the seal, and for no reason, closed it behind him. He repeated this process at the second seal and again at the final seal. Nearly exhausted, he closed and pressurized his suit, steeled himself and emerged to the surface in darkness beside the monitoring tower. One last climb and he would have a good view as the sun rose. His way lit by the suit's external lights, he cleared debris from the tower's ladder and began his arduous ascent to the top. By the time Roger forced the final platform open, there was a faint light in the east, familiar yet in eerie unfamiliar colours. Equally fatigued and stunned, he struggled to sit.

As the next hour passed, the light grew and the grave devastation lay before him. Simulated game world or not, it was heartbreaking. Not a sign of life, no water, just dust. He began to weep. Just then, one of the systems below, relaying through the tower, pinged him with a notification. He called it up on the suit's display screen.

`Happy 250th Birthday, Roger!`
`Have a GREAT day!`

CONTRIBUTORS

Ted Amsden was the third Poet Laureate of Cobourg. He is the editor of Cobourg Now and its sister sites in the News Now Network. Soon he will independently publish *The Golden Handshake Crew*, a comedy adventure about 60 seniors attempting to take over the town hall in a neighbouring town.

Kim Aubrey lives in Cobourg, Ontario. Her stories, essays and poems have appeared in journals and anthologies, including *Best Canadian Stories*, Event, Numero Cinq, Room and The New Quarterly. Her story collection, *What We Hold in Our Hands*, won an Honourable Mention in the Bermuda Literary Awards.

Heather Beveridge is a retired researcher and librarian living in Newcastle, Ontario who writes the stories of her ancestors as she finds them in her work as a genealogist. Published works include *Ancestral Spirits of Muskoka, a Memoir* and *The History of St. Thomas Anglican Church, Brooklin*.

Lynn C. Bilton has moved many times throughout Ontario. Each change of address has created an opportunity to meet a wonderful cast of new friends. She has had short stories published in three anthologies, plus numerous articles featuring her photography in *Our Canada* magazine. She now resides in Northumberland County.

mia burrus explores the boundaries and spaces between urban and wild, spoken and silent, fleeting and timeless, free-formed and structured, known and unknowable, mindless and mindful, through poetry, photography and bricolage www.miaburrus.com.

Christopher Cameron enjoyed a successful career as a professional opera singer, and in 2017 he published a memoir of his singing years, *Dr. Bartolo's Umbrella*. As editor of *Watershed* magazine and co-host of Word on the Hills, Christopher spends his days immersed in stories of the people and places of Northumberland County.

Michael Croucher has published two novels, one traditionally and one self-published. While work on his third novel is progressing slowly, he has been busy building a collection of short stories and narratives, which he plans to release in 2023.

Sharon Ramsay Curtis is a lover of words and an accidental writer. Her muse is quixotic and chooses her own time and space to make an appearance. Sharon's process proves to be untidy and unpredictable at worst and deeply fulfilling at best.

Susan Dwyer is a retired elementary school secretary who has also taught English in several International Schools. She belongs to a choir, a theatre group and lawn bowls. Susan has had several short stories published. She also facilitates a grief support group in Wilmot Creek, where she lives.

Antony Di Nardo's latest poetry collection, *Forget-Sadness-Grass*, was released in 2022 by Ronsdale Press. His book-length manuscript, *Through Yonder Window Breaks*, was winner of the inaugural Don Gutteridge Poetry Award and was published by Wet Ink Books. He was born in Montreal and lives in Cobourg.

Esther Sokolov Fine, York University Professor Emerita, Graduated University of Michigan, OISE, Vermont College of Fine Arts. Hopwood Award, Educational Press Association of America Distinguished Achievement Award. Recent publications: *Raising Peacemakers* (Garn Press), *Playing the Bully* (with J. Head, V. Shearham), poem in *We Are One* (Bayeaux Arts), *The Teacher's Helper* (upstreet, 2021-Pushcart nomination).

Katie Hoogendam (M.K./Merkat) is a poet, writer & interdisciplinary artist. Folklore, myth and the natural world inform her work. Her writing appears in publications across the U.S. and Canada. The selected poems first appeared in *Spring Thaw*, her third collection of poetry, published in March 2022 from Glentula Press.

Shane Joseph is a Canadian novelist, blogger, reviewer, short story writer, and publisher. He is the author of six novels and three collections of short stories. His most recent novel, *Empires in the Sand*, was released in September 2022. For details visit his website at www.shanejoseph.com

Wally Keeler is a performative poet utilizing photography, video and physical events to serve a creative narrative about the Peoples Republic of Poetry, a state of mind popularly known as the Imagine Nation. He has published in many literary journals here and abroad. Wally has been introduced as Canada's most dangerous poet.

Alan Langford has a wide range of interests that spans innumerable arts and sciences, with a particular interest in how technology shapes and is shaped by society. He can be reached at musing@alanlangford.ca.

Kathryn MacDonald's poems have been published in Canada, United States, Ireland, and England. Her poem "Duty/*Deon*" won the *Arc* Award of Awesomeness (January 2021). "Seduction" was shortlisted for the *Freefall* Annual Poetry Contest (Fall 2020). She is the author of *A Breeze You Whisper: poems* and *Calla & Édourd*, a novella.

Ronald Mackay has worked in many countries around the world, often at the most consequential times in their history. He has written about Tenerife, the largest of the Canary Islands and about living behind the Iron Curtain. He and his wife have lived on Rice Lake, Ontario, since 2012.

Alice McMurtry is a writer and museum professional. She has been a book reviewer with *Publishers Weekly* since 2014, focusing on speculative fiction. Her creative work is forthcoming in Cobourg's poetry newsletter *Poetry Present*. She enjoys writing short fiction and poetry. She lives in Cobourg.

Ken Morden lives in Cold Springs. After he had sold his marketing company in Toronto, he and his wife ran Oak Knoll Stables in Elizabethville, breeding Standardbred horses. They also owned dozens of racehorses over the past fifteen years. In 2021, he published a racing industry murder mystery *The Fraudulent Racehorse*.

Reva Nelson had several careers (by choice) including actor, entrepreneur and keynote speaker. She was the president of Words.Worth Keynotes & Seminars for over 20 years. Now a Cobourg resident, Reva's books are *Risk It!*; *Hippie Chick Abroad*, a memoir; and a book of poetry, *Twisted Branches*.

Jessica Outram is Cobourg's 4th Poet Laureate. She is a Métis writer and educator. For more information visit: sunshineinajar.com

Robert Pearson is a poet, an artist, and a long-time co-writer with the Northern Light Writers. Having left the urban hustle and bustle, he now enjoys a lake, a wilderness landscape, the silence of nature and the noise of the blazing sun setting behind a silhouette of granite and pine.

Marie Arden Prins lives, gardens and writes in Northumberland County, Ontario, Canada. Her middle-grade children's novel *The Girl from the Attic* was published by Common Deer Press in 2020. Her memoir pieces and poetry can be found on her website www.marieprins.ca.

Felicity Sidnell Reid's poetry, stories and reviews are published in anthologies and online collections. *Alone: A Winter in the Woods* was released by Hidden Brook Press, 2015. She is co-host/producer of the radio series on 89.7 FM, *Word on the Hills*. *The Yellow Magnolia*, her chapbook, was released in 2021.

James Ronson is the author of two novels, *Power and Possessions*, and *Blood, Fire and Ice*. This is his fourth time contributing to the *Hills Spirits* anthologies. James is planning to release his third novel, *Emperors and Hockey Ghosts*, in the fall of 2022.

Pam Royl's first novel, *The Last Secret*, will be published in the fall of 2022. A fervent lover of storytelling, she developed her writing skills through courses at the University of Toronto and under the mentorship of international award-winning author, Donna Morrissey. She lives in Northumberland County, with her husband Ian.

Gwynn Scheltema is published in anthologies, journals and magazines in Canada, Europe and South Africa, online and in print. Her poetry chapbook, *Ten of Diamonds*, was published in 2021. She's president of Northumberland Festival of the Arts, and co-host of *Word on the Hills* on Northumberland 89.7 FM . www.writescape.ca

Al Seymour is the author of three novels, a short story, several articles and is working on a historical fiction saga. He co-founded three charitable organizations and is a Cobourg Museum Foundation board member. He's working on the Foundation's dinner theatre play for fall 2022 and the museum's 2023 theme of immigration.

Susan Statham is an author and a visual artist. She is the editor for *Hill Spirits V* and co-editor and contributor for the previous Hill Spirits anthologies. *The Painter's Craft,* her first mystery novel features artist Maud Gibbons. Her second, *True Image* is complete and *Caged* is in progress.

Janet Stobie has written nine books—three short story collections, three children's books, two novels and one worship resource. You can check out her blog and her books at www.janetstobie.com.

Diane Taylor's first book was *The Perfect Galley Book*, a memoir about her life at sea. Her most recent book was *The Gift of Memoir,* a guide to writing memoir that she compiled while giving courses in memoir writing. She writes fiction, nonfiction and poetry.

Melissa Thorne has always loved reading and writing poetry. Only recently has she shared her own poetry with the public, participating in local poetry projects initiated by Cobourg's Poet Laureate, Jessica Outram. She's since been featured several times in Jessica's *Poetry Present* email series as well as published in the echapbook, *Cobourg Present*.

John Unruh is a Northumberland resident and writer concerned with the value of broken things and how communities come together to fix them. He is also a career technical writer and editor. You can reach him on Twitter @jtu_nwfrt or email at jtu@cogeco.ca.

Karen Walker writes in Cobourg. Her words are in or are forthcoming in *Bandit Fiction, The Disappointed Housewife, Reflex Fiction, Sledgehammer Lit, Funny Pearls, Versification, Unstamatic, Roi Fainéant Lit Press, The Ekphrastic Review,* and others. She/her. @MeKawalker883.

Catherine White, a new member of Spirit of the Hills, has been writing for some years. Her essays and short stories have been published in the *Globe and Mail, Transition,* a Canadian Mental Health Saskatchewan journal, as well as several online publications.

Donna Wootton is a graduate of the Humber School for Writers. Her book about her late father, *Moon Remembered,* is archived at Trent University. Her poetry was recently published in *The Divinity of Blue* and *Musings.* Her latest publication is the novel *Isadora's Dance* from Blue Denim Press.

OTHER TITLES IN THE HILL SPIRITS SERIES

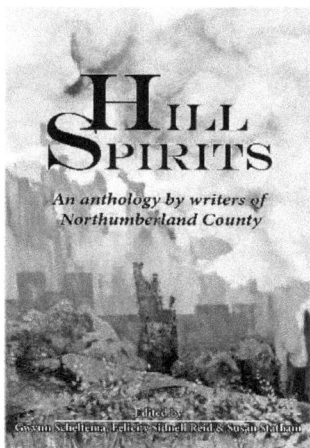

HILL SPIRITS
An anthology by writers of Northumberland County
Edited by Gwynn Scheltema, Felicity Sidnell Reid & Susan Statham

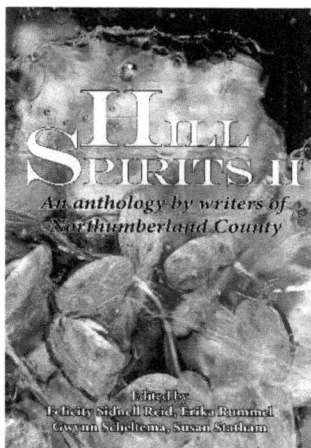

HILL SPIRITS II
An anthology by writers of Northumberland County
Edited by Felicity Sidnell Reid, Erika Rummel, Gwynn Scheltema, Susan Statham

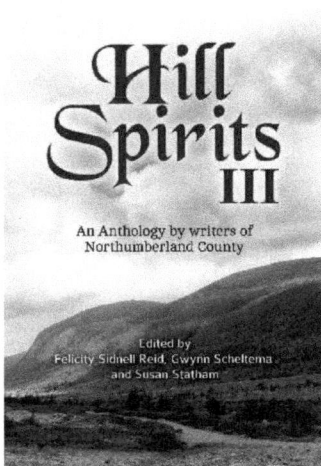

Hill Spirits III
An Anthology by writers of Northumberland County
Edited by Felicity Sidnell Reid, Gwynn Scheltema and Susan Statham

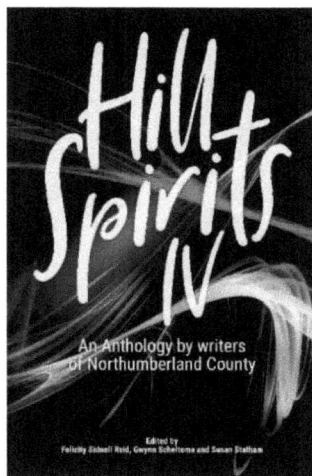

Hill Spirits IV
An Anthology by writers of Northumberland County
Edited by Felicity Sidnell Reid, Gwynn Scheltema and Susan Statham

Lightning Source UK Ltd.
Milton Keynes UK
UKHW020638151122
412232UK00017B/703